Caught in the Act

"How much time you think we have?" Shawn whispered.

Max shook his head. "Not much."

As they moved to join Adrian and Bobby, they heard the sound of approaching footsteps. Seeing a figure in a North Korean uniform facing the courtyard, they slipped further into the shadows.

Suddenly, the figure turned, coming directly toward them. They were trapped.

point

THE RESCUE

A Novel by Elizabeth Faucher
Based on the Motion Picture from Touchstone Pictures
Produced by Laura Ziskin
Based on the Motion Picture Written by
Jim Thomas & John Thomas
Directed by Ferdinand Fairfax

SCHOLASTIC INC.
New York Toronto London Auckland Sydney

ISBN 0-590-41532-8

© 1987 Touchstone Pictures
All Rights Reserved

Published by **Scholastic** Inc. POINT is a registered trademark of Scholastic Inc.

12 11 10 9 8 7 6 5 4 3 2 1   7 8 9/8 0 1 2/9

Printed in the U.S.A.   01

First Scholastic printing, November 1987

Chapter 1

It looked like any other U.S. Naval Air Base: a long row of fighter jets lined up along a flood-lit tarmac; low-storied barracks and supply sheds; chain link fences topped by concertina wire surrounding various guard towers and check-points. This particular military base was in Nae-Ri, South Korea, and was occupied by military personnel and their families. Families whose children had spent their entire lives growing up on Navy bases all over the world; their immediate surroundings always the same; the various states and countries always very different.

It was dark, a steady rain making the compound seem all the more anonymous. On top of one of the buildings, a figure dressed in black crouched near the edge of the roof, surveying the warehouses below through powerful binoculars. A soldier with a K-9 security dog was patrolling the area, and the figure in black moved into the shadow of an air shaft, out of sight. When the guard had passed, he lifted a tiny radio transmitter, pressing the mike key. After a short burst of static, he raised his binoculars, scanning the buildings until he saw another figure in black emerging from the shadows of a loading dock below.

The second intruder stayed very low, not moving, eyes sweeping the compound for movement. There was a static break on his transmitter, and he sprinted down the alley between two buildings, stopping in the shadow of a wooden utility pole.

He knelt down, taking a pair of single-spiked crampons from his belt and attaching them to his boots, clinching them tightly into place. Removing a rope from another belt hook, he whipped it around the pole, gripping an end with each gloved hand. He straightened up, dug his spikes into the pole, and began to climb up, hitching the rope a few inches higher with each step.

The other figure, still on the roof across the way, gathered up his radio and binoculars and ran to the other edge of the building, climbing down a steel staircase.

His partner swung from the utility pole onto another roof, dropping down out of sight. He checked the buckles on his climbing harness, then attached a carabiner to the metal ring on the front, hooking onto a support cable leading to a single-story building across the alley.

Just as he was about to slide down the cable, a patrol jeep cruised down the alley with its searchlight flashing. He froze, waiting for it to drive past, then let himself slide down the wires to the roof of the building below, landing with a small thud. He stuck a grappling hook on the lip of the roof, checked to make sure it was secure, then took hold of the rope attached to it, swinging over the side.

He rappelled down to an open ventilation window and gripped the edge of the sill, releasing the hook above him. It came plummeting down and he caught it and hooked it onto the sill. Then he slid inside the building to the floor far below. He snapped the hook and rope free, coiling the rope around his shoulder before creeping along the crate-crowded floor. He took a flashlight from his belt, shining it over a caged-in area in the far corner. It was stacked full of cases with military serial numbers, and he took out a small crowbar, snapping open the padlock on the cage door.

Above him, there was a small metal box

attached to the wall. He didn't notice the even smaller red light on top of it that began to flash.

Outside, alerted by the alarm, two jeeps filled with soldiers screeched to a halt in front of the building. Their leader, Gunnery Sergeant Davis, barked an order and the soldiers separated, moving to cover all of the exits. Some soldiers, holding weapons or leashed German shepherds, followed him inside, searching for the intruder or intruders.

Sweeping the perimeters, they converged on the cage, with its door swinging open, its padlock hanging loose.

Sergeant Davis played his flashlight over the cases. Two of them were obviously gone. "Looks like we just missed 'em," he said, then scowled, tossing the stub of his long-cold cigar aside. "Let's move! Double-time!"

The dogs followed a trail of wet footprints, soldiers bearing M-16's right behind them. The trail led to another, nearby building. The footprints stopped at a set of heavy, wooden accordion doors; light spilled out from underneath them. Instantly, reactively, the soldiers lined up in attack formation on either side.

"Kopenski, Nichols!" Sergeant Davis ordered two of the men. "Open 'em!"

The soldiers burst into the room, the attack dogs snarling at the ends of their

leashes, interrupting what had been a large
— and very loud — party. Teenagers, both
American and Korean, were dancing to a
jukebox, and on the far wall was a large,
hand-lettered banner reading:

"HAPPY BIRTHDAY, ADRIAN, SWEET 16."

Someone turned off the jukebox and the
teenagers stopped in mid-gyration, staring
at the guards, who were staring back. Sergeant Davis moved toward the group, focus-
ing on two boys who were distributing sodas
and beer from the two stolen cases.

A very attractive girl with short hair —
obviously Adrian, the guest of honor, since
she was holding a cake knife — sighed.

"Oh, *great*," she said, and lifted an eye-
brow at the two boys, both of whom were
still wearing their all-black cat burglar cos-
tumes.

The boys, Shawn Howard and Max Rothman, grinned sheepishly at each other. They
were both sixteen — Shawn, the handsome
jock-type, probably from the Midwest, Max,
thin and bookish, but still New York City
tough.

"Think we should rush them?" Max
asked, wryly.

Shawn shook his head. "I think they've
got us dead in the water."

Max nodded. "I think so, too."

Chapter 2

The next day a lone motorcyclist sped along the dusty road leading to the base. He was helmetless, wearing aviator sunglasses and a leather jacket with a colorful dragon painted on the back. He was seventeen, his hair cut in a short punk style, his expression tough and angry.

At the main gate, he weaved the bike expertly through the antiterrorist barriers, impatiently slowing down to let the guard recognize him.

"Slow it down, okay, J.J.?" the guard said, waving him through.

J.J. didn't answer, suddenly punching the accelerator and speeding into the base. He glanced down at his watch — late for school *again* — scowled, and drove faster.

At the high school on the base, Adrian and her best friend, Soon Hee, were in their karate class, going through their sparring exercises. Their instructor, wandering around to watch each set of partners practice, paused next to them.

Soon Hee moved forward with a combination of front kicks. Adrian retreated, sweeping the kicks away with rhythmic forearm strokes. Soon Hee adjusted, attacking with a series of front jabs, Adrian again expertly parried the blows, waiting for an opening. Then, as Soon Hee bent forward on a jab, Adrian snapped a powerful kick up, lightly hitting her stomach, following through with two front kicks and a spinning roundhouse.

Their instructor called out the points, and the bout over, Adrian and Soon Hee bowed to each other, speaking the Korean equivalent of "Good match."

"Adrian, you're still dropping your right shoulder when you step in," their instructor said as the bell rang. He clapped his hands. "Okay, everybody, that's it!"

Soon Hee and Adrian walked toward the locker room.

"I'm ready to go back to bed," Soon Hee said, smiling.

Adrian nodded. *"He's* worried about my shoulder dropping, and *I* can't even believe I made it in here today."

"Some party last night," Soon Hee said.

Adrian laughed. "Yeah. Glad my father's not around." She laughed again, opening the locker room door. *"Very* glad."

Outside, J.J. swerved his motorcycle into the school parking lot, dismounted and ran toward the main building. The corridors were quiet and empty, and he hurried toward his classroom, hoping to get there before anyone — a hand came onto his shoulder and he turned to see his first period teacher, Mr. Prestige.

"Well, that's three, Mr. Merrill," Mr. Prestige said, holding up his watch significantly. "The junior and senior classes are assembled in the gym. After that, I believe you know the procedure." He turned J.J. around, herding him in the direction of the gymnasium.

The gym was very noisy, students seated on the bleachers, everyone loudly discussing the possible reasons for this assembly. The principal, Mr. Dexter, stepped up to the podium in front of the bleachers, clearing his throat ineffectually.

"Good morning." He tapped the microphone, trying to get the students' attention.

"Could we take our seats, please? Everybody, please."

There was a feedback squeal from the mike and he winced; everybody else laughed. In the back of the room, Mr. Prestige escorted J.J. inside, indicating an empty space in the front of the bleachers. J.J. hesitated, Mr. Prestige gestured more emphatically, and J.J. walked up to the front.

Adrian and Soon Hee were sitting a few rows behind him and as he sat down, he caught Adrian's eye, not looking away until she did. Adrian frowned, then leaned toward Soon Hee.

"What a *jerk*," she whispered.

"Cute, though," Soon Hee whispered back.

Shawn and Max, the "cat burglars" of the night before, were seated further along the bleachers, with a crowd of jocks. Neither of them joined in the general horseplay, watching Mr. Dexter, worried about what he was going to say.

Mr. Dexter adjusted the microphone and tried again. "Today, students," he said, "we have a guest who has requested this assembly to speak with you. Afterward, you will go to your second period classes." He paused. "Students, the commander of the Nae-Ri Naval Air Station, Admiral Harold Rothman." Who just happened to be Max's father.

A hush fell over the students as Admiral Rothman stepped briskly over to the podium, his shoes mirror-bright, his dress uniform neat and crisp, covered with battle ribbons and decorations. Max sank lower in his seat.

A boy behind him pushed his shoulder. "Hey, Rothman, look who's here."

"We're *finished*," Max said to Shawn, who nodded.

The gymnasium was absolutely silent and Admiral Rothman — every inch the stern leader — surveyed the entire room before speaking.

"In case you have forgotten," he said, his voice both clipped and booming, "let me remind you that we are living in a foreign country, closely neighboring a Communist nation with whom we have been on the brink of war for well over thirty years. As a consequence, this base functions in a state of continual military preparedness, operating under strict codes of procedure that cannot, and *will not* be violated."

He paused, gazing around the room, none of the students meeting his eyes. "That code was violated last night," he said. "What may be regarded by some as a 'prank' could have resulted in disastrous consequences." He stared at them, to let that sink in. "As a reminder of the gravity of this intolerable behavior, your recreational activities are going to be severely curtailed — for an *indefinite* time."

There was a low grumbling. Max and Shawn sank even lower. Admiral Rothman's penetrating eyes came to rest on them, narrowing even more.

"And I assure you," he said, not looking away from them, "the individuals who instigated this breach of security will be appropriately dealt with."

Max and Shawn both smiled weakly.

Within a half hour, Max and Shawn found themselves standing in front of the school, each holding a two-week suspension slip. J.J. Merrill came shoving past them, also holding a suspension slip, which he crumpled and threw away before getting on his motorcycle. He fired it up, much more loudly than necessary, and Max and Shawn scowled at him.

"We hear you, stupid!" Shawn yelled, as the motorcycle roared out of the parking lot. He sighed, sitting down on the school steps. "Two weeks — I can't believe it." He sighed again. "At least my father's away on maneuvers."

Max didn't answer right away, catching sight of his mother leaning against their car in the parking lot, her arms folded, tapping her foot. She saw him, too, and motioned him over with one furious gesture of her hand.

"I wish my *mother* was on maneuvers," Max said.

Seeing her, Shawn nodded sympathetically. "I'm not looking forward to seeing mine, either."

Chapter 3

J.J. skidded into his driveway, parked the motorcycle in the garage, and slammed into the house. The furniture was all military issue, spartan and colorless, lacking any homey touches. He threw his jacket on the floor, then yanked the refrigerator open, grabbing a can of soda.

"If I can't discipline my son, how can I discipline my men?" an angry voice said from the living room.

J.J. froze, noticing a commander's cap sitting on the kitchen table. He swallowed and moved to the living room door, seeing his father standing across the room, just as lean as his son, his eyes hard and unsmiling.

"Why aren't you in school?" his father said.

Defiantly, J.J. drank some soda. "I thought you were on maneuvers."

"Once more," his father said through his teeth. "Why aren't you in school?"

"I – I got there late and they sent me home."

Commander Merrill moved his jaw. "How long, *this* time?"

"A week," J.J. muttered.

"Put down that soda," his father said. "Where were you last night?"

J.J didn't look at him. "I was around."

"Where *were* you last night; why weren't you at the Nelsons?" his father asked, not fooled. "I *said*, put the soda down."

J.J. hesitated, then set the can on the edge of a table. "I went into town."

Commander Merrill nodded, his jaw tightening. "You were ordered to quarters while I was gone, that bike was *not* to be touched, and the *deal* is that when I travel, *you* stay on the base with Commander Nelson's family."

"I stayed on the base," J.J. said defensively.

"Don't lie to me."

"I stayed for a while; what am I *supposed* to do?" J.J. asked, still afraid to look at him. "Hang around and watch television? You want me to go to the stupid Rec Room and guzzle punch with all the brats?"

"You know what I expect," his father said. "You've been back here for five months, and you've done nothing but prove to me you can't cut it. It's got to be by my rules."

J.J. let out his breath, sitting down on the couch. "Your rules are killin' me, Dad."

Commander Merrill shrugged. "If you can't hack the program, then we pack your bags and you can go stateside again and live with your mother."

J.J. looked up. "No way, man. You couldn't live with her, neither could I."

"That's unnecessary, mister," his father said.

"And *I* tried," J.J. said, even *more* unnecessarily.

Commander Merrill ignored that. "Then you'd better try *here*," he said.

J.J. shook his head. "I'm not interested in basic training."

"Well, you're in it, kid," his father said. "And *I* will make the decisions — you've got nothing to say about it. You want to take me on, let's go for it!"

J.J. jumped up, just as angry. "I never did have anything to say about it, about anything! Did I?" He gestured around the apartment, at the grey empty walls. "You call you and me a family? All you care about is how I stack up as a commander's son! Well, it doesn't mean *anything* to me that I'm a commander's son!" He knocked the soda can off the table with his hand, the liquid splashing everywhere, and stormed into the kitchen.

His father came after him. "What *does* mean anything to you?"

"Nothing you care about!" J.J. grabbed his jacket from the floor and ran outside, jumping on his motorcycle.

"You think I don't care about you?" his father yelled after him.

The motorcycle was already careening down the driveway. Commander Merrill watched his son speeding away, then sighed, rubbing his hand across his forehead. There was a knock on the front door and he went back to the living room, opening the door to a uniformed driver.

"Commander Merrill." The soldier handed him an envelope of sealed orders. "I have a car waiting for you, sir."

"Terrific." Commander Merrill sighed, looking in the direction of the kitchen and the back door; J.J. was long gone now. "That's — that's terrific."

Shawn hesitated outside his front door, not sure what he was going to find when he went inside. He took out the suspension slip, smoothed some of the wrinkles, and folded it more neatly before putting it back in his pocket. Then, he took a deep breath and opened the door.

The house was quiet, except for the grandfather clock chiming the hour in the front hall. It was a nice house, more comfortable and less military — which usually went hand in hand — than most of the other houses on the base. Mainly his mother's influence, although several walls and a trophy case were devoted to his father's military career. Photographs and mementos of his SEAL Team — a Navy Special Forces division — experiences: Vietnam; basic training; medals and ribbons and plaques; and other souvenirs of a military career almost two decades long.

On other walls and shelves, his mother had displayed Shawn's athletic career: varsity letters; trophies for football, basketball, baseball, and sailing; photographs of his accepting various prizes; sailing with his ten-year-old brother Bobby; winning R.O.T.C. awards. Pretty soon, Bobby would be winning his own awards.

Walking into the living room, Shawn saw his little brother lying in and around a nest of blankets on the couch. He was wearing pajama bottoms and an Iggy Pop T-shirt. He had a thermometer in his mouth.

"You still sick?" Shawn asked, checking around for signs of his mother.

Bobby took the thermometer out, examining it with more attention than it probably deserved. "Maybe," he said ominously.

"Where's Mom?"

"You'll see her soon enough," Bobby said. Ominously. Then, he grinned. "Two weeks suspension, huh?"

Shawn stopped. "How do *you* know?"

"Mr. Dexter called Mom. You're grounded for two weeks. You'll see, she'll say" — Bobby made himself look stern — " 'Don't worry, I've got *big* things planned for you, mister.' *And*, Dad wants to talk to you."

Shawn groaned. "*Dad?*"

Bobby nodded. "He's back."

"What about maneuvers?"

"They called them back to send them out again," Bobby said, shrugging. "Either way, you're dead meat. Mind if I watch?"

Their mother appeared from the kitchen, her hands on her hips, and Bobby quickly stuck the thermometer back in his mouth.

"Hey! Mom!" Shawn gave her a big smile. His *best* smile. "Hi!"

His mother didn't smile back. "I've already had a call from Mr. Dexter. You're grounded for two weeks, but don't worry, I've got *big* things planned for you, mister. *And*, your father wants to talk to you."

Shawn looked at his little brother, who grinned at him.

"What did I tell you," Bobby said.

Chapter 4

When Shawn's father, Commander Howard, came into the living room a few minutes later, Shawn pulled in a deep breath.

"Dad," he said, extra-casual. Extra-*cheerful*. "What's going on?"

Commander Howard, wearing his SEAL camouflage uniform, lifted one side of his mouth in a grin. "What's going on with you?"

"Your kind of stuff, Dad," Bobby said eagerly. "They almost pulled it off."

Their mother frowned at him. "Keep your mind on your health."

Commander Howard put his briefcase down on the coffee table, then ran a hand back through his hair, which was blond, and a little longer than a military commander's probably ought to be. "You sick again?" he asked Bobby.

Bobby put on a downcast expression. "*May*be."

Smiling, his father leaned down, picking him up in a hug. "How sick are you? Sick enough to take care of things while I'm off?" He lifted Bobby up higher, the muscles in his arms flexing. "I mean, you're a ninja, right? You can hold the fort."

Bobby flushed with pleasure at the compliment. "Before, you said we were going sailing this weekend."

"I'll take him," Shawn offered, leaning against the bookcase in the far corner of the room.

His mother whirled around. "I *told* you, you're grounded. Don't challenge me that way, Shawn, I don't like it!"

Shawn nodded, shoving his hands into his pockets. "Uh, where you going?" he asked his father.

Commander Howard put Bobby down. "Haven't heard yet."

Shaw grinned. "Is it something 'hot'?"

His father answered with a Don't-give-it-a-thought shrug. "Tomorrow, you go to school," he said to Bobby. "I'm not impressed by your getting sick every time I go away." He pointed a finger at Shawn. "And you're grounded. And you," he winked at his wife, "be here when I get back." He put his arm around her, the two of them walking toward the front door. "Shawn," he said over his shoulder, "take my bag outside, I want to talk to you."

There was a jeep, with the requisite military driver, parked at the curb. Shawn hung back near the front door as his parents said good-bye to each other. After they had embraced, Shawn's father motioned him over, and Shawn swung the duffel bag into the back of the jeep.

"Okay, sailor," his father said. "Whose idea was that last night? Max's, right? One of his brainstorms?"

Shawn nodded, kicking at the sidewalk with one sneaker.

"You could have been shot, you know."

Shawn nodded. It *had* been a pretty dumb stunt.

"Also," his father said, "for what it's worth, it doesn't do much for me, either, so how about some consideration for who we are on this base?"

Shawn nodded. "I'm sorry, we won't do it again."

"I'm just worried about what you're going to come up with *next*." His father gave him a hug. "Take care of your mother."

Shawn nodded. "Will you be back soon?"

Commander Howard grinned, giving him a thumbs-up sign and climbing into the jeep.

As it pulled away from the curb, Shawn moved to stand next to his mother and Bobby. His mother looked so unhappy that Shawn put his arm around her.

"He'll be back soon, Mom," he said.

She managed a smile. "Of course he will." Then, she shook her head. "Well. Come on, boys, let's go inside and fix some lunch."

It was lunch period at the high school, and most of the students were sitting outside on the grass to eat. A jeep pulled up in front of the building and Adrian's father, Lieutenant Commander Phillips, got out, dressed in his combat beret and camouflage uniform.

"Give me a minute, Wicks," he said to the soldier driving, who was also wearing camouflage fatigues.

"We don't have much time, sir," Wick said.

Lieutenant Commander Phillips nodded, scanning the crowded school yard, looking for his daughter. He spotted her and waved. Adrian immediately jumped up and ran over.

"Daddy!" She gave him a big hug. "You're back! You said another week."

"I'm back, but I've got to go out again." He held her away to look at her. "You cut your hair."

"Out again?" she said. "Where? Don't go again."

"Sorry, baby. I just — " He glanced at his watch. "I'm sorry, I've only got a minute.

How was the birthday party? Some wild bash, I hear."

Adrian shrugged. "Some big deal they made out of stealing some drinks, it's all stupid macho stuff." She hugged him again. "Do you *really* have to go?"

"Your hair *is* shorter," he said.

She laughed, hitting him. "Stop it, it's not shorter. How long will you be gone?"

"I don't know." He looked more serious. "Your mother said you had another run-in."

Adrian sighed. "Please don't leave me with her."

"You don't listen to her," her father said mildly.

"I *hate* it when you go like this," Adrian said. "We drive each other crazy — you know that."

Lieutenant Commander Phillips ruffled up her, indeed, very short hair. "Give her a chance."

Adrian shook his hand off. "She had one drink the other night, Dad, and she started in on middle age again, being all scared of it. *And* she's into that 'I should go to finishing school in Savannah' stuff."

"Okay, okay, calm down," her father said. "We'll talk about it when I get back."

"You *always* say that."

"I know." He nodded toward Wicks, indicating that he would be right there. "Look, just put on a dress for her once in a while, okay? Rain-check on the birthday dinner?"

"Sure, I — " Sensing a certain urgency in his manner, she looked at him anxiously. "Tell me what's up — is this some big deal?"

"It's always a big deal," her father said, shrugging. Then, he pulled her over for another hug. "You're my girl, right? Trust me."

"But, is it anything — "

"I love you." He released her, heading for the jeep. "Give your mother a break, okay?"

"Okay. Be careful," she added quietly, as the jeep pulled away. She was still standing there long after it was gone.

Chapter 5

Within an hour of being alerted, the Special
Forces officers — Merrill, Howard, Phillips,
and Wicks — were assembled in Admiral
Rothman's office. Admiral Rothman stood
before them, in front of a very detailed,
tactical map of Korea. The map was broken
into grids and vectors in various colors,
dotted with code numbers and symbols.

"Five hours ago," he said, his expression
very grim, "a Los Angeles class sub had an
explosion in her engine compartment. Source
unknown. Their electrical and propulsion
systems were severely damaged. They're dead
in the water." He picked up a pointer, showing the position on the map, a spot in the Sea
of Japan near the North Korean coast.

"Here." He turned back to face his officers. "That sub must not fall into enemy hands. I want your team on deck in thirty minutes." He picked up some sealed orders, handing them to Commander Howard.

"Yes, sir." Commander Howard saluted, then looked at the other officers, who were all poised to move. "Full briefing in the air, men."

The assault plane was a C-130, flanked by two helicopters. They took off from the Nae-Ri airstrip, passing over the coastline and heading out to sea, staying very low in the air to avoid radar detection.

Inside the cargo hold of the C-130, J.J.'s and Shawn's fathers led the briefing. The SEAL team, in scuba gear, gathered around a large Plexiglas grid map. The other two SEALs held smaller Lucite tactical boards, copying down the information with grease pencils.

"So, what about the crew?" Commander Phillips asked.

"They surfaced, and most of them were transported to a Japanese trawler," Merrill said. "The captain and three officers are still on board. A tug's on the way, and they've submerged to periscope depth, shut down all systems."

"Problem's the Musu Dan Current," Commander Howard explained, pointing to the map. "At their present drift rate, they'll be inside North Korean waters in less than two hours."

Wicks looked up from his tactical board. "Any bad guys around, skipper?"

Howard nodded. "They've already got a fix on her. Ships, ASW choppers, the works." He smiled grimly. "They're waiting."

"What about the sub?" Wicks asked.

"We blow it," Merrill said.

When the pilot's voice came over the intercom, the SEAL team was ready.

"Approaching target," the pilot said. "Stand by for deployment."

As the plane banked into a turn, the SEAL team stood in prejump formation, their static lines clipped into the jump rigging of the aircraft. The "Alert" lights on the bulkhead were flashing red, and as the warning light changed to yellow, the soldier who served as loadmaster released the lock on the rear cargo door.

Slowly, the cargo door swung open, revealing the rushing ocean below. As the yellow light changed to green, the plane powered into a sixty-degree climb, nearly standing on its tail. Another soldier, the jumpmaster, activated the pallet, which would release the double parachute carrying the rescue raft.

The double parachute snapped open and the jumpmaster turned, giving the signal to stand by, and then jump. In perfect timing, the SEAL team raced to the rear of the plane, jumping in tight formation.

Their sky-blue parachutes descended around the larger double parachute, heading for the dark water below. Once they were deep in the water, the black hull of the twenty thousand ton submarine loomed above them, submerged, just below the surface.

The SEAL team glided down the forty-foot-tall conning tower to the entry hatch, Merrill extricating a small black electronic receptacle from his scuba suit. He flipped the switch that activated it, and there was a rapid burst of high speed code as the hatch opened, revealing the flooded chamber. Merrill, Howard, and Wicks entered, while Phillips stayed above water with the rubber rescue boat.

He covered the boat with protective netting, then took his binoculars from a watertight case, checking the horizon. There was clear sea on all sides, the raft pitching wildly on the grey swells.

Below, the submarine captain and his officers — located swiftly by the SEAL team — exited the entry chamber, ascending to the surface. Seeing them, Phillips picked up his radio, speaking into it.

"Joshua-1, Joshua-2," he said crisply, "We have the football. Repeat, we have the football." He clicked the mike off, turning to help the captain and his crew into the boat.

"What about *your* men?" the captain asked, out of breath.

Phillips shook his head. "My orders are to get you out of here as fast as possible. Please go."

A small speck in the distant sky came closer, and within moments the lead rescue helicopter swung into position, the propeller wash churning the sea into white froth as the 'copter hovered just above the boat. Phillips helped them climb aboard, remaining in the boat to wait for the rest of the SEALs.

Below the water, Howard, Merrill, and Wicks moved along the massive hull of the submarine, planting high-explosive magnetic charges and switching the detonators to "On." Finished, they regrouped and Merrill pushed a button on the master detonator attached to his wet suit, starting a thirty-minute countdown. A small red light on the detonator began to blink, indicating that the devices were armed and the countdown had begun. Then, the men dropped their scuba gear, making an unencumbered ascent to the surface.

Phillips helped them into the boat, pointing to the horizon, where the second rescue helicopter was approaching.

"Joshua-3," he said into his radio, "we have you in sight."

"Power up so we can move into position," Howard said, his voice urgent.

Phillips nodded, turning on the engine as the helicopter came closer, back-lit by the sun. Suddenly, the helicopter made a hard turn away from them.

"What — " Merrill started, stopping as they saw a North Korean gunship bearing down on them, enemy soldiers training an electric Gatling gun and other machine guns at them.

Phillips let out his breath. "Oh, boy."

Merrill nodded. "Big trouble," he said and the four men slowly raised their hands.

Chapter 6

Word of the capture came back quickly to the base, but that was the *last* quick thing that happened. Hours turned into days, which turned into weeks, which turned into a month. A *month.*

It was night and Adrian sat on the floor in her living room, her arms wrapped tightly around her knees. The only light in the room came from the television, flickering as a news broadcast began.

Behind her, in the kitchen doorway, stood her mother, a delicate Southern woman, definitely not suited to the military life. Hands trembling, she lit one of her many cigarettes these days and stared at the television set.

"The continuing drama of four U.S. Navy servicemen, charged with espionage, moved into its thirtieth day," the television announcer was saying, "the men are being held in a remote prison camp near the DMZ."

As pictures of the four men — pictures she had to see day after day: formal Navy portraits — flashed on the screen, Adrian clenched her fists in frustration. She turned to ask why someone didn't *do* something, *anything*, but stopped herself as she saw silent tears running down her mother's cheeks.

Clenching her fists more tightly, Adrian turned back to the television, very close to tears herself.

J.J. was in a pool hall in Seoul, the room dimly lit and smoky. It was a rough hangout, filled with merchant marines, enlisted men, and Korean waterfront workers. Alone and angry, J.J. had come to the pool hall often lately, playing game after game of eight ball, taking on anyone who wanted to challenge him, happy to take them on in a fight afterward — win or lose.

The nightly news was on the television above the bar, and J.J. leaned on his cue stick, watching. Men in the pool hall were discussing the incident all around him, their opinions loud and agressive, and he scowled at them.

"Turn it up!" he yelled.

A man reached up, raising the volume.

"Controversy still rages over the incident," the newscaster was saying, "the Communists insist that the captured men were engaged in espionage against their country and will be tried as spies. The trial, to be held in the capital city of P'Yongyang, could begin as early as next week. . . ."

"Hey!" One of the hoods J.J. was playing with pushed his shoulder. "Take your shot."

J.J. scowled, shoving him away with the cue stick. "Count me out," he said, and forced his way through the crowded room, out into the night.

At Admiral Rothman's house, Max was in his bedroom, hunched over his desk. It was cluttered with papers, soft drink cans, computer hardware, and other small mechanical gadgets. He peered through a magnifying drafting light at the gutted remains of a transistor radio, soldering components and wires to a small circuit board, about the size of a cigarette pack.

Beside him, a small portable television was tuned to the news, and he paused to watch for a minute.

"Mounting outrage throughout the country had led to rumors of direct military intervention," the announcer said, "but the White House and the State Department continue to pursue the release of the men through diplomatic channels — "

Max turned the set off in disgust.

"Yeah, right," he said to the blank screen. "Thanks for the disinformation." He bent back over his project, connecting a pair of earphones to the radio and putting them on.

At first, there was only static and he adjusted a few connections, finally hearing voices. He listened intently, then his eyes widened.

"*Wow*," he said and turned the volume up to listen some more.

In the Howards' living room, Shawn and his mother sat on the couch, watching the news. Bobby stood near his father's trophy case, his arms limp at his sides.

"The President," the announcer said, "referring to the prisoners as 'hostages,' has called the trial a 'sham;' simply 'an arena for propaganda.' However, if tried and convicted, the men, under North Korean law, face execution."

Shawn closed his eyes, his mother covering her face with her hands.

"We go now," the announcer said, "to the U.S. Embassy in Seoul South Korea, and foreign correspondent, Bob Waterfield. . . ."

"This guy's a jerk," Bobby said, his voice shaking. "I've seen him before — he's a real jerk."

Mrs. Howard reached for him and he burst into tears, trying to pull away. She hung on, holding him tightly as he sobbed into her shoulder.

"Turn off the television, Shawn," she said, her voice exhausted. "Just — just turn it off."

Chapter 7

The next day, Adrian and Shawn went to a nearby diner for hamburgers, Bobby coming along to occupy himself with video games. Adrian and Shawn waited at the front counter for their food, both of them too tired and sad to be very hungry.

"They're not even *trying* to get them out," Adrian said. "It's just a lot of 'diplomatic' junk."

Shawn rubbed his hand across his eyes, more and more tired. "They're trying — they'd *have* to be."

"Oh, yeah," she said. "Trying *real* hard."

"How's your mother taking it?"

"Straight up," Adrian said, then shook her

head. "Thirty days. The Israelis would've had them out *twenty-nine* days ago."

Shawn sighed, since they'd been having this argument for days now. "Have a little faith."

Adrian nodded, sarcastically. "There you go, God and country."

"What's the matter with that?" Shawn asked. "You have to believe in *something*."

Their food arrived and they carried it over to the condiment stand.

"Like what happened with the MIAs?" Adrian asked, squirting some ketchup on her hamburger. "I *still* have an uncle somewhere in 'Nam. What about Lebanon? What about Iran? Face it, they don't know what to do. They thought Grenada was, like, some *big* victory." Angrily, she squirted more ketchup on her plate, for the French fries. "Big *deal*."

"Hey, come on, take it easy," Shawn said. "What are you, some kind of expert?"

"Take it *easy*?" Adrian said, turning to stare at him. "Your father's stuck in some prison somewhere — don't give me power and glory."

"You don't have to tell me where my father is, *okay*?" Shawn said, his voice rising.

Adrian picked up her plate, carrying it over toward the nearest table. "Yeah, well, don't believe in fairy tales, because maybe they'll kill him. Kill all of them."

Shawn followed her, scowling. "So go see the President, why don't you?!"

"I'd do a better *job*," Adrian said and sat down.

They sat in tense silence, neither of them eating, and finally, Adrian put on a smile.

"Well." She lifted the top part of her bun to look at the greyish hamburger. "At least their food can't be worse than *this*."

"Trouble with *you*," Shawn said, "is, you don't trust anybody."

"Not the person who made this *sandwich*."

Shawn shook his head. "They just need more time, that's all."

"Another *month*?"

"I wish you wouldn't scream all the time," he said.

"You don't have to be afraid of me — I'm just a girl," she said, the last bit mocking.

Shawn shook his head, picking up his hamburger.

Max came into the diner, his jaw frenetically working on a wad of bubble gum. He looked around, saw them, and hurried over.

"We need to talk," he said.

Shawn shrugged, less than excited. "What's going on?"

Max glanced around to make sure no one was listening, then lowered his voice. "I think they're going to try a rescue."

Adrian's head snapped up. "*What*?"

"Where'd you hear that?" Shawn asked, just as eager.

"I bugged my father's study," Max said. "He was telling my mother."

"Wow," Shawn said.

"It's great!" Adrian said happily. "*You're* great!"

Max produced a small bug from his pocket, not noticing Bobby heading toward them. "See, I used my Walkman. Hooked the mike to the radio, added a couple of things." He stopped, putting the bug in his shirt pocket. "Shawn, I don't want your brother in on this."

"Hey," Bobby said, nodding at Max. "What's going on?"

"Sorry, kid, private conversation," Shawn said.

Bobby sat up on the table, with apparently no intention of budging. "About what?"

"If it's private, what's the difference?" Max asked.

Bobby looked at Shawn. "Is it about Dad? If it's about Dad, I want to know about it."

"It's private," Shawn said. "Bug off."

Adrian stepped in. "Bobby, it's not about your father, okay?"

Bobby hesitated.

"Really," she said, and handed him a couple of quarters, indicating the video machines. "Here."

Bobby hesitated some more, but backed away.

"Go on," Shawn said, when he was out of earshot.

Max checked to make sure he really *was* out of earshot. "If I get caught. . . ."

"You won't get caught," Shawn said.

"Go *on*," Adrian said, impatiently.

Max pulled a chair over, sat down. "There's a big meeting this afternoon at my father's office. Half the State Department's here."

"Will they tell us what they're going to do?" Adrian asked.

"What, are you kidding?" Max took out the bug. "I have a plan."

Shawn nodded, catching on. "Your father's office?"

Max smiled. "Yeah."

"Yeah, but, how can you do it?" Shawn asked. "How do you plant it?"

Max smiled, blowing a slow bubble. "Don't worry," he said. "I have a plan."

Chapter 8

Max walked into base headquarters, seeing high-ranking officers and important-looking civilians everywhere. Outside, Bobby sat on his BMX bicycle, having followed Max over; no one noticed him in the confusion.

Max headed for his father's office, nervously chewing his gum. It had been turned into a briefing room, with a large conference table and several covered easels, overhead projectors being rolled in next to them. As Max entered the room, he stopped, seeing an officious CIA type just finishing an electronic sweep of the room for bugs. He nodded at Max's father, then gathered up his equipment, Max stepping aside to let him pass.

Admiral Rothman looked up from a stack

of thick folders. "Max, what are you doing here?"

"Well, I — " Max swallowed. "Could I see you a minute, Dad?"

His father shook his head, annoyed. "I don't have a minute — you should have called. What is it?"

"It's, uh, personal."

"Well, make it quick," his father said impatiently. "Is something wrong? Your mother?"

"No, sir." Max looked around the room, chewing his gum, reaching into his back pocket.

Admiral Rothman let out an irritated breath. "Take that gum out of your mouth."

"Yes, sir." Max removed it, putting his hands behind his back and mashing the gum onto the back of the bug.

His father folded his arms. "You aren't in more trouble?"

"No, sir." Max walked over to the table, leaning against his father's desk, trying to anchor the bug to the underside.

"Then, will you get to it, son?" his father said sharply.

"I-I know I've screwed up lately," Max said, and pressed harder on the edge of the desk. On the *gum*. "I'm here to tell you that I'm not interested in trouble anymore. I'm here to tell you, sir, how I feel about myself lately."

His father's eyebrows went up. "Oh?"

"But you're busy, sir, and — "

"I'm extremely busy," his father said, "but let's get into this tonight. I'm glad you stopped by."

"Yeah, I — well, see you tonight, Dad." Max started for the door, but then noticed the bug starting to fall off. He went back to the desk, catching it just before it fell.

Admiral Rothman looked up from the folders. *"Now* what?"

"I — " Max thought frantically, pressing the bug on more securely. "I want to go to the Naval Academy, Dad."

"You *what*?"

Max nodded. "Yes, sir. I've been thinking about it since our men were taken, and my inclination has been to serve my country, sir. My feelings have sort of gone that way in the last month."

His father looked very pleased. "Well, now, you're on the move, aren't you, boy? You know how happy it'll make your mother to know you're on your way to the Academy."

"Yes, sir," Max said.

"If nothing else good comes out of this terrible thing, at least this will."

Max pasted on a smile. "Yes, sir."

"Not everybody gets to know so clearly the moment they stopped being a kid and started being a man," Admiral Rothman said.

Max nodded. "Thank you, sir."

His father smiled at him, and raised his right hand in a salute. Max smiled weakly and saluted back.

Outside, Max ran across the parking lot to the hangar where he'd set up a listening post on the second floor. Shawn and Adrian were already there, listening to a large radio-cassette recorder.

"Does it work?" Max asked.

"Yeah, the meeting just started." Adrian gave him an enthusiastic hug. "You're a genius!"

"*Gentlemen, Secretary Gates,*" they heard Admiral Rothman saying over the radio.

"Who's Gates?" Adrian whispered, not that anyone in the meeting would have been able to hear her.

"Assistant Secretary of State," Shawn said. "Now we're getting somewhere."

"*In front of you,*" Admiral Rothman was saying, "*you have a classified secret briefing incorporating recent intelligence from our operative in North Korea. Captain Miller will continue the briefing with an update on Operation Phoenix.*"

"Miller's the SEAL commander for Westpac; he's been to my house and everything." Max grinned. "He's scared of my mother."

"If they're using Westpac, that *does* mean rescue," Shawn said.

44

Max nodded, listening.

"*Gentlemen, Secretary Gates,*" a new, very formal male voice said. "*Operation Phoenix is ready to be implemented, coinciding with the Workers' Festival, six days from now. We have a secret, direct route into the fortress, part of the penetration already accomplished by our contact. Despite the heavy security, by exploiting this weak link, the rescue has a high probability of success.*"

Up in the listening post, they all cheered.

"Go get 'em!" Adrian said.

"Shut up," Max said, waving his hands for them to be quiet. "Listen!"

A new, and very grim, voice broke in. "*Bob, let me stop you for a minute. . . .*"

"Who's that?" Shawn asked.

"Has to be Secretary Gates," Max said. Adrian nodded.

"*We're all familiar with the operation,*" the Secretary was saying. "*But I think we have to address the larger picture, and the international complications involved.*"

"*International complications . . . ?*" Miller asked.

"*We can't prove our men were in international waters when they were taken,*" Secretary Gates said.

"*You* know *they were,*" Miller said. "*We all do.*"

"*Bob, we can't prove it, and besides, it doesn't mean a thing to the North Koreans.*

They're playing this to the hilt — they've really got us up against the wall with this one." The Secretary paused. "At this juncture, a rescue attempt is simply not justifiable. Our only option is to continue to negotiate."

"What are they doing?" Adrian whispered, horrified.

"My men were taken in international waters," Admiral Rothman was saying, sounding incredulous, "and under Article fifty-one, we have every right to go in there and get them."

"You bet we do," Shawn said. Max and Adrian nodded.

"The President was with us before," Admiral Rothman continued, "why the change?"

"Harold," the Secretary was speaking again, "the President is outraged about this incident, outraged. If it were up to him, he'd be in there himself — you know that. But the way things stand with North Korea and her friends, the President is just unwilling to pull the trigger."

"You have to pull the trigger!" Shawn yelled at the tape recorder. "You have to!"

"Our only recourse," the Secretary said, "is through diplomatic channels."

"For the next week" — Miller was obviously speaking through his teeth — "we've got an open window; the only chance we've got to go in there and get those men. *If we lose this opportunity, they don't stand a chance — they're as good as dead."*

Up in the hideout, Shawn was trembling. "They're not going to do it. I don't believe it."

Adrian just stared at the radio. "They've GIVEN UP?"

"I'm sorry, gentlemen," Secretary Gates said, *"but under the circumstances, Operation Phoenix is out of the question.*

In the hideout, it was silent for a few seconds, then Adrian started crying.

"You're traitors!" She yelled at the radio. "You're all COWARDS and TRAITORS!"

Chapter 9

Shawn walked Adrian home, both of them
still shaken by what they had overheard —
and *now* fighting about whether or not J.J.
Merrill had a right to know about it. Bobby
was trailing behind them on his bicycle, but
they ignored him.

"We *have* to tell him," Adrian said.

Shawn shook his head. "I'm telling you,
the guy's a loser — he's not one of us. He'll
just screw things up."

"He's one of us *now*," Adrian said, stopping
as they got to her front walk. "He has a *right*
to know."

Shawn shook his head, fists tightening at
the very *thought* of having a conversation
with J.J. Merrill.

48

"Hey, we need all the help we can get — I can't worry about *your* personal hang-ups with him." Adrian turned on her heel, walking up to her front door, then inside.

Shawn watched her go, still shaking his head.

Bobby rode closer, his attitude too casual to be convincing. "What's going on?" he asked, looking innocent.

"Will you *stop* following me around?" Shawn moved past him and down the street. "Go home already!"

J.J. sat on the floor of his garage, working on his motorcycle. Not that there was any thing wrong with it — but working was better than sitting around waiting for news bulletins.

Trying to remove a nut, his wrench slipped and he winced as his knuckles glanced off the metal. He reached for his toolbox, searching for a larger wrench, but paused, looking at the small photograph wedged inside the cover. It was a picture of him when he was five, peering out from underneath one of his father's caps, smiling proudly. There was also a SEAL Team decal pasted on the cover, with the imprinted SEAL slogan on the bottom: WE TAKE CARE OF OUR OWN.

There was the sound of a door opening behind him, and he turned to see Shawn Howard, whose expression was both stubborn and pugnacious. As always, Mr. King of the Jocks.

"What do *you* want?" J.J. asked, standing up.

Shawn tossed a cassette tape onto the nearby workbench. "I think you should hear this."

J.J. shrugged, bending over the motorcycle engine. "What is it?"

"It's about your father," Shawn said. *"Our* fathers."

As Shawn walked out, J.J. stared at the tape, then slowly picked it up. He brought it into the house, his Walkman lying on the kitchen table. He studied the unmarked tape for a minute, then snapped it in, putting on his earphones.

He listened with growing horror, all the while looking at the framed picture of his father that was sitting on the counter. He rewound the tape to listen again, then set his jaw, reaching for the phone to call Shawn.

Shawn had suggested meeting in the deserted hangar after dark that night, and J.J. agreed. Stumbling a little in the blackness, he found the back stairway, following it up. He opened the door at the top of the stairs, and saw Shawn, Adrian, and Max sitting around a small table.

J.J. frowned, gesturing toward Max. "What's *he* doing here?"

"He's a friend," Shawn said calmly.

"*His* father isn't even over there."

"*My* father's responsible," Max said, just as calm as Shawn. When J.J. still didn't come in, Max nudged Shawn. "Tell him I made the tape."

"He made the tape," Shawn said.

J.J. moved his jaw, considering that, then leaned against the doorjamb with his arms folded.

"Yeah, you're all so macho," Adrian said, and turned to face J.J. "Shawn and I want to go to Washington, talk to people. We've scraped up enough money from savings — Max, too — if you want to put in, you're welcome to come."

"Who do you talk to when you get there?" J.J. asked, looking bored.

"Anyone who'll listen!" Adrian said.

Shawn nodded. "We start with the newspapers — "

"Oh, *please*," J.J. said, and shook his head.

"Hey," Shawn got up angrily, "if you came up here to blow us out of the water — "

Max interceded, his voice very calm — and more like his father's than he wanted it to be. "I think the President would see them — he likes that stuff."

"Sure he would," J.J. said, his voice patronizing. "And he'll pat you on the head, tell you how brave you are, and break the hearts of

America. But you *won't* change their minds."

"Yeah, well, we can't just let them die in there without trying *something*," Adrian said.

Max said. "I don't know. I guess we *should* put the money back."

"No!" J.J. said quickly. "We might need it."

They all looked at him and for the first time, he smiled.

"I have an idea," J.J. said, and reached into his jeans pocket, taking out a small golden crest. He held it up as though it were some sort of amulet. "We all know what this is?"

"Yeah, the SEALs' crest," Shawn said. "So what?"

J.J. read the inscription. " 'We take care of our own.' "

They all looked at him.

"Yeah," Adrian said, finally. "So?"

"That's us." J.J. tapped on the crest, then on his own chest. "The family. Except this time, they won't let the SEALs take care of their own."

Shawn shook his head, half irritated, and half interested. "What're you getting at?"

"They've written them off." J.J. snapped his fingers to punctuate. "And you're just going to sit back and be one of the numbers? Or are you going to do something? *Really* do something?"

"Like what?" Shawn asked doubtfully.

J.J. smiled again. " 'Operation Phoenix.' "

"Wait," Shawn said. "You mean, *we* go get them?"

J.J. nodded.

Chapter 10

"I *love* it," Adrian said, already on her feet. "Let's do it!"

"Unh-unh, no way." Max shook his head. "We can't."

"Why *not*?" J.J. said, with a definite figures-*you'd*-be-chicken note in his voice.

"The word 'death' comes to mind," Max said.

"Let him talk, Max," Shawn said, leaning forward on his arms.

"It's all there for us," J.J. said, looking at Shawn. "The plans, the agents, everything."

"Hey, yeah," Adrian said. "You're right!"

"But, wait." Shawn frowned. "How do we get the plan?"

J.J. looked at Max. Significantly.

Max shook his head. "Unh-unh, not me. I'm not going to be responsible for your lives."

J.J. brushed that aside. "Can you figure a way into Miller's quarters?"

Max shook his head. "No."

"You *know* you can," Shawn said, pushing him. "Come on, Max."

Max sighed. "My father will buy an electric chair. My *mother* will pull the switch."

"So you'll do it?" J.J. asked. "Figure something out?"

Max nodded.

Outside the hideout, in the shadows of the staircase, Bobby crouched in the darkness, listening to everything that was being said.

It was very late, and softly, a ventilation grate in the officer's quarters swung open. J.J. and Shawn, dressed in dark clothing and sneakers, dropped noiselessly to the floor. Then, they looked up at the open vent in the ceiling, their hands extended.

"Okay, drop it!" Shawn whispered.

A dark athletic bag hurtled down, landing between the two of them with a crash. Max stuck his head out of the vent, shaking it in disgust.

"Nice one, guys," he whispered.

Shawn and J.J. scowled at each other.

"Why didn't you catch it, stupid?" Shawn asked.

"I thought *you* were going to catch it," J.J. said. "*Jerk.*"

They had climbed into a room with an empty bed and a nightstand and, hearing footsteps out in the hall, they both froze. The steps paused outside the door — probably a guard on duty — then continued down the hall.

The boys exchanged looks of relief, then moved over to the nightstand, where a briefcase was resting. The name on it read: Captain R. Miller, U.S.N.. As J.J. picked up the case, it was yanked out of his hands, but Shawn caught it just before it hit the floor. He pulled on the handle, then saw that the case was handcuffed by courier-chain to the bedframe.

He mouthed the words "Now what?", and J.J. pointed to the door leading to the bathroom. He picked up one end of the bed, Shawn followed suit and, straining with the effort, they carried it across the room.

J.J. motioned for Shawn to hold the briefcase, rear edge facing out, then took an aerosol can of Freon propellant from their duffel bag, along with several tools. He turned the bathroom light on so he could see what he was doing, then sprayed the hinge joints of the case with the Freon. The spray froze the joints, turning them white, and J.J. placed a small chisel against the bottom of the hinge pin. Then he covered the end of a hammer with a rag, and hit the chisel sharply, knocking free the crystallized metal ends on both hinges. Using a nail, he quietly tapped out the hinge pins, then lifted off the lid of the case.

A thick file was sitting on top, with the words — stamped in red — across it: CLASSIFIED: TOP SECRET USN PACCOM, PHOENIX. He showed it to Shawn, and they both smiled.

Max had managed to get them a hand-held copy machine, and Shawn spread out each page of the file, one at a time, while J.J. ran the copier over them, a huge mound of paper forming on the floor behind him.

"This is the last roll," J.J. whispered finally, checking the copy machine. "Get the maps, blueprints, and the name of the contact. Forget the rest."

Shawn nodded, and searched through the file.

"We don't have much time," J.J. whispered.

Shawn nodded, and searched more quickly.

In the hideout the next morning, they cut the massive roll of copier paper into sections — like film strips, almost — and pinned them to the walls. Max sat on the floor, taking the pieces one at a time, trying to fit together the various maps, documents, and codes. Whenever he had one completed, he would tape it together and hand it to one of the others, who would hang the completed document on the far wall.

J.J. stood in front of a taped blueprint, studying the information, a pencil between his teeth.

"Looks pretty clear cut," Adrian said. "They really had it organized."

J.J. turned to Shawn, ignoring her. "The big problem is finding this operative, Kim Song. And if we're going to make it, we've got to go tomorrow night."

"The *big* problem," Shawn said, "is getting us a boat."

"Don't worry about the boat," J.J. said, with a confident wave. "I've got a guy in Seoul. If the money's right, I can do it. You bring the money?"

Adrian turned to Max. "Give him the money."

"Hey, wait a minute," Shawn said, holding his hand out to stop Max from coming over. "Who is this guy with the boat? Can we trust him?"

"You got a better idea?" J.J. said. "You want to call the yacht club?"

Shawn stood his ground, the two boys facing each other. "Maybe I should. We don't know this guy."

"Just give him the money," Adrian said, sounding very tired.

Max pulled a wad of bills out of his pocket,

setting it on the table. "That was my new amplifier," he said wryly.

"Okay," Adrian said, and J.J. picked up the money, counting it. "Then we go tomorrow night."

J.J. stopped counting. "*You're* not going."

Adrian stared at him. "What?"

"We can't take her," J.J. said to the other two. "It's hard enough what we have to do without having a *girl* around. It's too dangerous."

Max and Shawn looked at Adrian, waiting for the fireworks.

Adrian stepped up to J.J., furious. "*Look*, buster." She jabbed him in the chest. "Just who do you think you are? It was *my* idea to bring you in in the first place! My *money's* in there! My father's *up* there! I'm as much a part of this as any of you." She pointed the same finger at Shawn. "*Any* of you. And I'm *definitely*"—she jabbed J.J. again—"going."

"All right, Ace!" Max said, and clapped.

"Okay, she's going," Shawn said quietly.

"She's *not* going," J.J. said.

"She's going!" Shawn said, and this time, J.J. didn't argue.

Chapter 11

Before meeting the others the next night, J.J. sat in his father's bedroom, thinking. The plan might not work. In fact, the odds were — he went over to his father's footlocker, smashing the padlock open with a hammer. He reached down inside the footlocker, taking out a polished walnut case. He opened it, removing a .45 automatic, his father's name inscribed on the barrel. He hesitated, then stuck the gun in his waistband, grabbing two magazines of ammunition. Then he looked at his watch and got up to go.

Bobby, wearing his darkest clothes and a baseball cap and carrying a small knapsack, coasted down Adrian's street on his bike. He braked silently just beyond her house and hid the bike in some bushes. Then, he crouched down, watching as Adrian lugged a duffel bag over to the trunk of her mother's car — known around the base as the Wedge. As she returned to the garage, Bobby darted out of the bushes and slipped into the trunk, closing the lid behind him.

Back inside her parents' garage, Adrian turned her attention to Max, who was sitting uncomfortably on a wooden chair as she applied lipstick and makeup to his face.

"Hold still, Max," she said impatiently. "You're not going to get through the gate without this — you have to look *something* like my mother." She stepped back, examining her work.

"How bad is it?" Max asked.

Adrian made a face. "At least it's dark out." Digging into a brown paper bag, she handed him one of her mother's dresses and a well-padded brassiere.

Max groaned, accepting them. "This better not ever get out."

Adrian laughed. "You'll always be a hunk in my book. Just be careful with the Wedge — my mother loves that old car."

"What if she catches me when I bring it back?"

Adrian shook her head. "I told you, she puts the news on and stares at the TV all night, waiting for the next catastrophe."

"I hope you guys aren't it," Max said. "We're talking about life and death here."

"Nobody's going to die," Adrian said, making her voice confident. "Get dressed. I'll be right back."

She went upstairs to her parents' bedroom, where her mother was coming out of the shower, a towel draped around her hair, wearing a bathrobe.

Mrs. Phillips stopped, startled. "What is it, Adrian?"

"I'm going out," Adrian said.

"Oh." Her mother started drying her hair. "Don't be late again, all right?"

"Okay." Adrian turned to go, then turned back. "Momma, I love you."

Now, her mother looked really startled. "Well — that's nice, darling."

Adrian turned to leave again, then came back. "No, Momma, I mean I *really* love you."

Mrs. Howard reached out to touch her daughter's hair. "I love you too, sweets."

Adrian kissed her mother's cheek, and swiftly left the room.

The main gate of the base was brightly lit as Marine guards checked incoming and exiting traffic. Max, wearing heavy makeup, a sunhat and sunglasses, slowed the Wedge down, its muffler blaring away.

"Well, here goes," he said, the other three quiet and tense. He took a deep breath and pulled up next to one of the guards, keeping his head down.

"Evening, Mrs. Phillips," the guard said politely.

Max put on a sweet Southern drawl. "Evenin', corporal."

The guard stepped back, waving the car through, and Max stepped on the gas.

The Seoul waterfront was crowded and noisy, the cobblestone streets jammed with bicycles, rickshaws, vendors, and hustlers. Max drove the Wedge very slowly, since people were reluctant to move out of the car's way, and gave these obvious outsiders long, hard stares.

No one in the car spoke, all of them nervous and preoccupied by the enormity of what they were about to do. Adrian, in the front seat, looked back once and her eyes met J.J.'s. They held the stare for a brief, tense moment, then Adrian faced forward.

Max guided the car down a dark, mist-filled alleyway, very close to the docks.

"Is this it?" he asked.

J.J. nodded. "This is it."

They parked in a rundown section of rotting wharves and warehouses. A light fog drifted across the water, the disintegrating sampans, junks, and water taxis. Their car was at the end of a dilapidated pier, its rotting pilings supporting a deck of broken and decayed timbers.

There was another pier across from them, with a floating restaurant and attached dock. They sat in the darkness, listening to the faint music and noise from the building. And they waited. And waited.

It was twelve-thirty and J.J. stood outside the car, holding a pair of binoculars. Adrian and Shawn slouched on the back of the car, while Max — still in drag — paced back and forth.

Max stopped, looking at his watch. "Look, guys, this has been really *swell* and all, but I've had it. If they were supposed to be here at nine — well, let's face it. They're not going to show up."

No one else spoke.

"If that's not getting through," he said, "then watch my lips: We've been *ripped off*. Let's just kiss the thousand bucks good-bye and get out of here."

"Two thousand," J.J. said quietly. "They took it all."

"What! You spent all of it?" Shawn lunged over to him, grabbing his shirt in one hand. "I should've known better than to trust you and your slimeball connections!" He got into the driver's seat, slamming the door. "Come on, let's get out of here."

Max nodded, moving to get in, too. "Now

you're making sense." He paused, seeing that Adrian hadn't budged. "We'll think of something else, Adrian, don't worry."

Reluctantly, she slid off the trunk, still looking at J.J., who was staring out across the water.

"Come on, Ace," Shawn said. "Just leave him."

Hearing the muffled roar of an engine, J.J. raised his glasses, seeing a black speedboat entering the light cast by the floating restaurant. He watched as the boat pulled up alongside the dock, where a similar boat was tied up. Zooming in with the glasses, he saw three Korean men jump from the boat, quickly unloading some boxes. Other men came out to help them, one of them brandishing an automatic weapon. As one of the men turned in their direction, J.J. was able to see him full-face. He lowered the binoculars.

"That's him," he said quietly. "That's the guy."

Chapter 12

Adrian took the glasses from him, surveying the scene, seeing a lot of dangerous underworld types coming and going from the restaurant.

"You bought a boat from *them*?" she said, handing him back the glasses. "I'd say it's a no-money-back deal."

J.J. raised the glasses, training them on the empty speedboat. "Maybe so, but they *still* owe us a boat." He handed the binoculars to Shawn. "You're the sailor, can you drive that hog?"

Shawn looked at it through the glasses. "Sure, tough guy. We just gonna go ask them for it?"

J.J. shook his head, taking him seriously.

"We'll have to sneak over there and do it."

"Do it?" Max said. "You're just going to go over there and *do it*?"

J.J. tossed him the binoculars. "You got a better idea, boy genius?"

Max scanned the area, then looked at Adrian. "Is the Wedge insured? Collision, that stuff?"

"Two hundred deductible," Adrian said. "I think."

Max tossed the glasses back to J.J., looking at him defiantly. "Then no problem."

Adrian caught on. "Now, wait a minute, you guys — "

"Trust me," Max said. "*I* know what I'm doing." He shot a look at J.J., then got into the car.

Max parked the Wedge, with its engine running, so that the car was aimed at the entranceway of the restaurant. He opened the hood and wrapped a piece of wire around the accelerator linkage, locking the carburetor *wide open*.

"Better idea," he muttered. "Boy genius." He closed the hood, wiping his greasy hands on the front of his dress, then checked the tension of the two ropes tying the door handles to the steering wheel.

J.J., Shawn, and Adrian were in position at the far end of the lower level of the restaurant, hiding behind some crates and boxes.

The speedboat was at the end of the dock, where one of the Korean smugglers was using a hand-cranked pump to top off the boat's gas tanks, a submachine gun slung over his back.

J.J. looked at his digital watch, thirty seconds showing. He got up, the others following him.

Max looked at his digital watch, the timer reading twenty seconds. He leaned over the car door, putting his hand on the key. Then, from the rear of the car, he heard a dull thumping. Frowning, he walked back to the trunk. There was more thumping and hesitantly, he opened it, jumping back as something popped out at him.

It was Bobby, wearing his own version of commando garb and smiling uncertainly.

"I don't believe this, Bobby!" Max hauled him roughly out of the trunk. "What are you *doing* here?!" The beeper on his watch went off, and he groaned. "All right, all right, stick with me! It's show-time."

The alarm still sounding, he reached inside the car, turning the key. The engine roared, accelerating wildly. Max jammed the gear shift into low, and a cloud of blue smoke and burning rubber erupted from the back tires as they spun on the wet pavement. Then, the tires caught and the Wedge, a four-thousand-pound guided missile, leaped forward.

Max jumped out of the way, dragging Bobby with him, and started to run away down the street. But Bobby broke free, racing after the speeding Wedge. Max spun around, running after him.

"Come back here, you little jerk!" he yelled.

Hearing the roaring engine, the smuggler on the dock looked up, his back to J.J. and the others, who were creeping up behind him. Hearing something else, he turned as all three of them rushed him, knocking him out of the boat and into the water.

Above them, the Wedge hit the front door of the restaurant, smashing inside. J.J. cast away the boat's mooring line as Shawn turned on the engine. J.J. leaped over the windshield, into the cockpit.

"Come on!" he shouted over the crashing noise of the Wedge as it demolished the inside of the restaurant.

Bobby, with Max in hot pursuit, tore along the upper level as Korean hoods, molls, and patrons dove through the windows and doors of the restaurant, trying to get out of the way of the speeding car.

For a minute, J.J., Shawn, and Adrian stood in the boat, staring up at the debris raining down from the restaurant.

"The whole building's coming down," J.J.

said, awed, then recovered himself. "Let's go, let's go!" Hearing a noise, he glanced behind them. "Look out!"

Shawn and Adrian turned and saw that the smuggler had pulled himself up onto the gunwale and, while balancing on one knee, was aiming his AK-47 right at them.

Chapter 13

For a second, they were all stunned. Then,
with a loud karate yell, Adrian delivered her
best spinning roundhouse kick, knocking the
man back into the water. Amazed by the success of the kick, she watched him flounder in
the water.

"I did it!" she said. "Did you see that?"

Shawn, his hands on the throttles, looked
up, his mouth falling open as he saw Bobby
running toward the boat. Max, his dress
pulled high, was right on his heels. Bobby
flung himself into the boat, Max followed
close behind, both of them landing on Adrian.

"Bobby!" Shawn said, stunned. "How — "

"Go, *go*, GO!" J.J. yelled.

Shawn reacted then, slamming the twin throttle controls forward, the force of the acceleration knocking all of them to the deck.

Adrian pointed, seeing the other speedboat heading toward them from the other side of the dock. "Hit it, here they come! Everybody down!"

The smugglers in the other boat opened fire, bullets ripped into the boat, smashing the windshield.

"Move it, Shawn, move it!" Max said, completely panicked.

Shawn crammed the throttles as far forward as they would go, the boat surging ahead. The other boat stopped, the smugglers aiming the machine guns, ready to cut them apart. Just then, in an explosion of glass and splintering wood, the Wedge crashed out of the restaurant, heading out across the water.

The smugglers dove out of their boat as the Wedge smashed into it, disappearing in a geyser of water, steam, and flying wood.

"We did it!" J.J. yelled, throwing one fist into the air.

As Shawn piloted the boat through the light fog, the others looked back at the destroyed restaurant and the tail fins of the Wedge slipping beneath the water.

"You know something?" Adrian said, her voice shaking a little from the strain of the last few moments. "My mother's going to be pretty upset about that."

* * *

It was late that night, and a government sedan screeched to a halt in front of the naval base headquarters. Guards rushed to open the doors, escorting Mrs. Howard and Mrs. Phillips out. Both women, looking distraught and exhausted, were taken to Admiral Rothman's office, where Mrs. Rothman was waiting for them. Where they *all* could wait for Admiral Rothman.

"What I don't understand," Mrs. Rothman said, sitting on the edge of her husband's desk, "is who could have talked my Max into doing this thing."

Adrian's mother sighed, lighting a cigarette. "Well, it *was* Shawn and Max in the last episode."

Shawn's mother put her hand on her hips. "Virginia, if you're implying that Shawn influenced Max — "

"I'm not implying anything," Mrs. Phillips said. "It could very well have been Max's idea — he *did* plant the bug. But, more than likely, it's that J.J. Merrill who instigated it. I very much *doubt* that it was Adrian."

"Who cares who instigated it?" Mrs. Howard snapped. "Our children could be dead, for all we know. Virginia, do you *have* to smoke?"

Mrs. Phillips inhaled deeply. "If there's one day I need a cigarette, Sybil, it's today."

"Well, blow it in a bag or something," Mrs.

Howard said, waving the smoke away with an agitated hand.

Admiral Rothman came in and sat down behind his desk.

"Did anyone call J.J.'s mother?" his wife asked, frowning at him.

Admiral Rothman nodded. "I did, but she wasn't in. I had to leave a message on an answering machine."

"Well, you should send her a cable, then," she said.

"I *did*, Vella." He looked around the room, taking all of them in in one glance. "Now, I understand what's going on in all of us, myself included. But we're doing what we can, we're covering the borders. I will contact you with *any* small piece of information we get."

Mrs. Phillips lit another cigarette. "Is that all we're doing, *covering borders*?"

Admiral Rothman sighed. "Virginia, we're doing what we can. We'll find them."

"*Find* them?" Mrs. Howard said, her voice ragged. "Why are we even *in* this situation? Why wasn't there a rescue attempted *before* this? Why were you so belly-frightened to go in there and bring out our men in the *first* place?"

"He had every intention of rescuing those men, Sybil," Mrs. Rothman said angrily. "It wasn't *his* decision not to."

Admiral Rothman hit his desk with his

fist. "Vella, please!" Then, he spoke more calmly. "This kind of thing is not going to bring any of them back." He paused. "Please. There's only one thing we can do now, and that's to hope we reach those children before they cross into the North."

Chapter 14

It was dawn the next day, and the speedboat motored quietly into a magnificent river canyon, its steep rock walls shrouded in low-lying clouds. Shawn was at the wheel, an open map at his side, a tiny flashlight protruding from his pocket.

The others sat quietly, Bobby alone in the back of the boat, his eyes wide and scared beneath his baseball cap. Shawn cut the throttle and turned off the engine, the boat rising up and down in the light swells.

The only sound was the water, lapping against the sides of the boat.

"That it?" J.J. whispered, breaking the silence.

Shawn nodded a very small nod.

"Look clear." J.J. coughed, his voice gaining strength. "Let's go."

Shawn didn't move, staring straight ahead.

Adrian got up, her legs stiff from sitting. "What's the matter?"

"We're not going," Shawn said. "I can't take Bobby in there."

"Shawn!" Bobby protested. "I can take care of myself."

Shawn whirled around. "*You* shut up. You've got nothing to say about this. Messing up everything, following me around!"

"I'm not here to follow you!" Bobby said. "I'm here to get my dad."

J.J. climbed to his feet, giving Shawn a hard shove. "What d'you mean, we're not going? We're not gonna turn the boat around and go back, if that's what you mean."

Shawn shook his head, apparently not even noticing the shove. "He'll never make it in there. I don't know if *we'll* make it in there."

"I made it *this* far," Bobby said, defiantly.

"I don't even want to argue about it," J.J. said, focused on Shawn. "He's a little brat — but he's here. We're *not* turning this boat around."

"I'm not taking him over," Shawn said. "It's too dangerous."

Max, still sitting, cleared his throat. "He has a point, that's not North *Dakota*."

"Hey, you crossed that line last night," J.J. said. "Why didn't you say something then?"

Adrian moved up the front of the boat, putting her hand on Shawn's back. "Shawn, we had a plan."

"And he wasn't part of it," Shawn said stubbornly.

Bleary-eyed, Max rubbed his hand across his forehead. "Look. Maybe we should take a vote."

"I said I'm going, and I'm going." J.J. pointed at Adrian. *"She's* gonna go." He looked at Max. "You don't *have* to go, you don't have a father in there." He looked to Shawn. "You don't *want* to go, so take your brother and the three of you get off now, go ashore while it's still safe, make your way back."

Adrian sighed. "Don't do that, J.J., we have to stay together."

"Hey, you don't like it," he said, "you go, too!"

Bobby sat down, folding his arms. "I'm not leaving the boat."

Shawn yanked the key out, closing it inside his fist. *"Nobody's* leaving the boat."

J.J. tried to grab it from him. "We don't have time to fight about it."

Shawn closed his fist more tightly, holding it out of J.J.'s reach. "You're not giving the orders around here."

J.J. looked at him, sneering. "You know what you are, you're scared, you're chicken, you're hiding behind your baby brother — "

"He's not chicken!" Bobby said.

" — because you don't have the guts to go in and get your father," J.J. went on. "Well, maybe you don't care about *your* old man, but I care about mine — I'll go in there myself if I have to, and if I don't die doing it, I'll bring him back, and if you're such a chicken and want to go home, I'll bring yours back, too!"

Shawn jumped on him, fists swinging, while Max and Adrian tried to break it up, and Bobby hit J.J. from behind.

"Cut it out!" Max shouted. "Just cut it out! We can't think about it anymore; we just have to go — we just do it — we go, all the way — the plan — the commitment — all of it — all our lives — us — your fathers — me — all of us — we all come back or we all don't — bottom line — let's cross it right now — *do it* — *NOW, before I know what I just said!*"

They all looked at Max; then they all looked at Shawn.

"*You*," Shawn said to Bobby, "lie down on the bottom of this boat and *don't* move." He stared at the canyon looming ahead, then started the engine, pushing the controls forward.

Slowly, they moved up the river, entering North Korea.

* * *

Up the river, some distance away, a Korean officer in a patrol boat lifted his binoculars. Seeing the black speedboat, he lowered them, turning to the boat's pilot.

"Smugglers," he said in Korean. "Full speed ahead."

Chapter 15

They rode slowly up the river, Shawn and J.J.
scanning the water ahead of them for movement, Max and Adrian keeping a careful
watch from the rear. Bobby sat on the deck,
his head below the sides of the boat, out of
sight.

Suddenly Adrian gasped. "Look!"

Max stared, too. "Oh, no, we've had it!"

The powerful patrol boat was coming up
behind them, with what appeared to be an
officer watching them through binoculars.
Other men on the boat were running to take
their positions behind heavy machine guns,
as a loud siren began to wail.

Shawn jammed the throttles forward and
their boat picked up speed.

"Get down!" J.J. ordered. Everyone but Shawn hit the deck.

The patrol boat opened fire, a hail of bullets churning up the water all around them. Shawn, trying to keep his head down, twisted the boat in a series of evasive turns, trying to lose the other boat *and* avoid the bullets.

Adrian lifted her head just enough to see over the stern. "They're gaining on us, Shawn."

"I can't outrun them!" Shawn yelled, the throttles open all the way.

"Well, do *something!*" Adrian yelled back.

Shawn looked around frantically, then saw a narrow tributary to their right. "Okay, hang no!" He yanked the steering wheel so hard that the boat went out of control, spinning in a complete circle, nearly throwing all of them out of the boat.

Recovering, Shawn yanked the wheel the other way, steering the speedboat toward the narrow tributary. There was yelling from the patrol boat, which careened after them. Shawn rocketed the boat down the narrow watercourse, while low overhanging branches slapped against the hull and windshield.

"Here they come!" Max said.

Shawn powered the boat through a sharp turn, flinching as he barely missed hitting the rocky canyon wall. Trying to outmaneuver the other boat, he cut through several shallow patches, forcing the larger patrol boat to stay in deeper water. But, passing over one shallow spot, there was a sickening crunch from somewhere underneath the boat.

"What was that?" J.J. yelled.

"It wasn't good!" Shawn yelled back.

The patrol boat was still firing at them, bullets ricocheting wildly off the rock walls on either side. Shawn whipped through the canyon, managing to swerve past a jutting rock, but the patrol boat took the turn less successfully. The rock sheared off part of its side.

Ahead of them was a sluice-bridge— a manmade series of gates to control the flow of the river water. A group of workers was in the process of lowering the gates when, alerted by the sound of gunfire, they looked up, seeing the boat chase. As the patrol boat fired indiscriminately, the workers abandoned their jobs, running for cover on the nearby riverbanks, leaving the last gate only partially closed.

"Oh, help," Shawn said quietly, seeing the seemingly solid bridge ahead of them.

Behind them, the commander of the patrol boat smiled. "They're trapped," he said.

Approaching the bridge, Shawn started to slow down, avoiding a rock jetty. Then, he saw the partially open gate and pushed the throttle out all the way.

"Get down!" He yelled, as the boat screamed through the gate with barely an inch to spare.

The commander of the patrol boat shouted for his driver to follow, but as they got closer to the gate — and it was more obvious that the bigger boat would never squeeze through — they all jumped overboard. The patrol boat smashed into the gate, bursting into flames.

Hearing the explosion as they sped to safety, Shawn and the others turned to look, cheering as they saw the roaring fireball leaping for the sky. Shawn guided the boat around one more bend and then, out of sheer exhaustion, shut down the engine.

The only sound was Adrian crying.

"Hey," J.J. said, touching her shoulder. "You all right?"

She looked up, her eyes bright with excitement, and he realized that she was laughing. He stared at her, then started laughing himself, the others slowly joining in until they were all in hysterics.

"We made it," Shawn gasped, laughing weakly. "I can't believe we made it."

After a while, they began to calm down, except for Max, who was laughing so hard that there were tears in his eyes.

"You all right, buddy?" Shawn asked.

Max pointed to the rear of the boat, where water was swiftly seeping in — from bullet holes, or rock holes, it was hard to tell.

"Welcome to North Korea, everyone," he said, and laughed. "What next, dude-commandos?"

Chapter 16

As the boat sank, they salvaged what they could and made their way to the riverbank.

"Now what?" Shawn asked, squeezing some of the water out of his shirt.

J.J. shrugged. "Push on."

It was the best idea anybody had, so they worked their way along the riverbank, through thick green vegetation, trying to be as quiet as possible. They had been walking for what seemed like a very long time when J.J. — who was in the lead — stopped.

"Look." He indicated a small fishing village, just up ahead.

There were a number of pole-house shacks built right at the river's edge, and the villagers were seated on their porches, smoking, conversing, having a midday meal.

"I'm starved," Bobby whispered.

Shawn looked worried. "Maybe we could ask — "

"Oh, yeah," Adrian said. "I'm sure they'll be *thrilled* to see us."

They all looked at Max, who was silent, studying the group of sampans, small, flat-bottomed skiffs, and larger fishing boats.

"Got a plan?" Shawn asked him.

Max nodded. "Yeah. Think I do."

None of the villagers noticed, but a series of bubbles surfaced alongside the sampan staked furthest away, then a head — Shawn's head — broke through the surface. His hand came up, holding a Swiss Army knife, and carefully he cut through the mooring line. Then, the head and hand disappeared; the sampan slowly, almost imperceptibly, edged away from the bank.

Other hands came out of the water, removing sets of black peasant clothing, hung on rails along the riverbank to dry. . . .

Later they were all in the sampan, heading up the Tae-Dong River. Shawn, wearing a peasant outfit and hat, sat at the tiller, warily watching the water ahead for trouble. In the bow sat the other four, wearing black peasant outfits and mismatched hats. Max was asleep, his hat low over his eyes, while J.J. watched the riverbanks and Bobby watched his brother. *Proudly* watched his brother. Adrian leaned back against the side of the boat, staring up at the awesome beauty of this forbidden land, as the tiny sampan made its way up the magnificent river canyon. The only sound was the low *putt-putt* of the little outboard engine.

As dusk came, a light mist floated across the tranquil surface of the water, the remaining sunlight transforming the scene into a softly glowing, dreamlike world. J.J., now at the tiller, turned off the motor, and the sampan floated along in complete silence. Somewhere far away, there was the lonely, haunting cry of a waterbird, which echoed across the water.

"Wow," Bobby said.

"Unbelievable," Adrian said, her voice just as hushed.

The other three nodded, staring at this strange and unfamiliar country, so beautiful that it was hard to imagine the danger lurking within.

As the sun set, they pulled the sampan up along the riverbank, hiding it under thick bushes hanging out over the water. By the time the boat was securely moored, it was dark, and Max and Shawn built a small fire. The two of them sat by it, talking in low voices, Bobby lying half-asleep a few feet away.

J.J. and Adrian sat by the water, very quiet, looking up at the bluish-black sky, with brilliant stars spread across it.

"Same stars as we have," J.J. said softly.

Adrian nodded, her eyes on the sky. "I keep imagining my father. I keep seeing him looking at me when I come for him." She shivered a little. "I wonder what he'll say."

"I know what *mine'll* say," J.J. said.

Adrian looked at him, away from the sky. "What?"

J.J. put on his father's sternest expression. " 'Why aren't you at the Nelsons?' "

They both smiled at that, then didn't speak for a minute. J.J. shifted his position, ending up somewhat closer to her.

"You know, you did great back there," he said. "I was real proud of you, the way you took out that guy."

Adrian blushed slightly, then laughed. "*Tell* me about it — I didn't even drop my shoulder! I couldn't believe it, I was so — I felt like I could've taken on an army."

J.J. smiled, and it was quiet again.

"This the first base you've lived on?" Adrian asked.

J.J. shook his head. "I've been in" — he counted them off on his fingers — "Greece, Florida, Guam, and then the Bronx with my mother." He grinned wryly. "*That* was the hardest duty." He glanced over at her. "What about you?"

"I don't know, all over," she said. "Home-towns galore. I was born in Kansas, then straight to Puerto Rico. Germany. Alaska."

J.J. nodded and they looked at the stars, listened to the quiet river. Adrian broke the silence.

"Do you believe somewhere inside you that nothing terrible is going to happen to us?" she asked.

He didn't answer right away. "No," he said finally.

Adrian nodded, trying to smile. "C-crazy, isn't it?"

"Nothing's crazy," he said, watching the river.

It was chilly now that the sun was down, and Adrian wrapped her arms around her-self. There was a small crackle in the bushes and they both jumped, but the sound went away, leaving the riverbank quieter than ever.

"Truth is. . . ." Adrian swallowed. "I'm really scared."

J.J. looked at her, then slowly extended his hand, taking hers. "Me, too," he said, and tightened his grip. "Me, too," he said, almost whispering.

Chapter 17

The sun rose over the prison camp, which looked peaceful and calm. The camp had been built high above the Tae-Dong River, and the rising early morning mist made it seem all the more peaceful.

However, the prison commandant was standing on the prison terrace, watching impassively as guards shoved Commanders Howard and Phillips from the interrogation room, back toward the cell compound. Both men were thin and bruised, but defiant, doing their best not to cooperate as the guards forced them along.

Phillips was pushed into his cell first, landing on his knees on the thin straw pallet their captors had provided as bedding. The tiny cell was dark and cold; the guards slammed and locked the heavily rusted metal door. The cell was pitch-black, except for a stripe of light where the food access slot was. The damp cold walls led upward to a ceiling of iron bars, occasional harsh light flooding the cell from the searchlamps above.

Feeling his way along the floor, Adrian's father dragged the filthy pallet over to the corner, huddling up on it to try and stay warm.

Further down the hall, J.J.'s father was locked in his cell, sitting on the floor with his knees pulled up to his chest. His skin was sickly-white, his eyes vacant hollows of torment and stress. But despite the dark bruises on his face — from precise, repeated beatings — his determined expression made it obvious that his spirit hadn't been broken.

Hearing the slam of the adjacent door, he straightened up.

"Howard?" he called hoarsely. "You all right?"

In the hall outside, there was shouting in Korean, running footsteps, then the rattle of keys as his cell door crashed open. As two guards stormed in, Merrill froze, staring straight ahead. The guards screamed at him, brandishing their bayonets in his face, kicking him toward the wall.

Merrill stared straight ahead, refusing to acknowledge their brutality, and they finally left, the door banging closed. He grimaced and slowly rolled over onto his back. Gripping the piece of mortar he'd chipped out of the floor days before, he began to tap out a soft Morse code against the cell wall, once again stubbornly trying to contact his fellow prisoners.

As the sun rose higher in the sky, Shawn cautiously navigated the sampan through the traffic of other river crafts, the wakes from passing boats making it a bumpy ride. They had rigged up a piece of canvas as a sort of roof over the boat, and everyone except Shawn was able to stay out of sight.

Rounding a bend, they saw a high palisade overlooking the approach to a floating city, its height and ruggedness more than a little ominous.

Bobby peered out from the canvas at this new and exotic world. "Where are they, Shawn?"

Shawn pointed to the jagged cliffs. "Up there, somewhere." J.J. and he exchanged an uneasy look, and Shawn focused back on the river, steering to avoid both collisions and detection.

Well into the harbor, he guided the small boat toward an inlet, the engine sputtering and popping, steering the boat deeper into the other water traffic.

Passing through the inlet, the sampan

emerged into an Asian Venice, an endless array of sampan houseboats and stilt shacks, connected by a maze of canals and passageways.

"Think they can see us?" Max muttered, well under the awning.

"I'm not sure," Shawn said, careful to keep his head lowered so that none of the river people would see that he was a foreigner. "Just stay down."

The sampan glided past a guard tower, where a soldier was keeping watch on the river traffic. Shawn bent the brim of his hat, hiding his face, and J.J. — who had come out to help navigate — bent over, pretending to mend a fishnet. As they drifted past safely, both boys let out their breaths.

"Whew," J.J. said, and Shawn nodded, wiping his sleeve across his face.

Under the awning, the others studied the river course carefully, comparing landmarks called out to them by Shawn and J.J. with information on their photocopied Operation Phoenix plans.

"We're coming up on a turn," Shawn said anxiously. "Which way?"

J.J. leaned toward the awning. "Which way, Max?"

"I don't know," Max said, sounding nervous. "Try — the right."

J.J. leaned back. "Make a right."

Shawn hesitated. "You sure?"

"Absolutely," J.J. said, and blinked a couple of times.

Shawn turned the boat into a narrow waterway, lined by buildings. From the look — and the smell — it seemed to be a fishery. Shawn cut the engine, letting the sampan drift over to a landing bay. Although there were racks of fish around, the area was completely deserted.

Max poked his head out, Adrian and Bobby surfacing more cautiously. He looked at one of his photocopies. "This should be it. Last one on the right."

Adrian frowned, looking both ways. "There's supposed to be a signal. Clothing on a line. Blue, red, yellow — "

"Plan's canceled, remember?" J.J. said. "Nobody's expecting us."

"This place gives me the creeps," Bobby said, and Shawn patted him on the back.

J.J. stepped, with catlike silence, onto the landing, motioning for the others to follow. They crept into the fishery, which was crowded with cutting tables, racks, and chopping blocks. The walls were lined with long tanks filled with live fish; the room was softly lit by sunlight that streamed through high windows, barely making it to the floor.

There was a door at one end of the room and slowly, J.J. pushed it open, peering inside. It was empty, except for a table, and as they stepped inside, they saw a still-smoldering cigarette. J.J. put his fingers to his lips, approaching another doorway, and they all froze as the barrel and silencer of a Russian automatic was shoved under his jaw. A peasant riverman, dirty and grease-stained, stepped out from the darkness, pushing J.J. up against the wall.

Another man stepped out of the shadowy doorway, pointing a silenced machine pistol at the others.

"Look, uh — " J.J. gulped, the gun pressed right into his throat. "Who are you? We're looking — are you Kim Song?"

The man jabbed the pistol into his chest, not answering.

"Do you understand?" J.J. asked, his voice shaking. He lifted his hand, revealing the SEAL crest. "Operation Phoenix. *Phoenix*," he said, trying to make the man understand.

The other man released a catch on the table, rotating it to one side, revealing a stairway. He motioned with his gun for them to move and hesitantly, they started down the stairs.

"I don't think these are the right men," Bobby whispered.

Next to him, Max nodded. "I think we're in *big* trouble."

Chapter 18

They were led into a basement room, dimly
illuminated by oil lamps. On one wall, a bank
of high-tech radio receivers and tape re-
corders were in the process of being dis-
mantled; on the other wall, there was an
arsenal of weapons, including machine guns,
rocket launchers, and hand guns. The two
Koreans taking apart the radios were placing
the parts in boxes, which were then covered
by false tops filled with dried and salted fish.

Adrian nudged Max. "They're talking
about the Operation. Something about — "

A large man in his mid-forties stepped out
into the light. He had an air of quiet authority
as he scrutinized them, his eyes piercing.

"We're looking for — " Adrian started.

"*I* will talk," the man said sharply, in almost unaccented English. He studied them for a long minute, then stabbed his finger at Bobby. "Who are you?"

Bobby gulped. "Robert Franklin Howard, sir!"

The man's expression didn't change. "How old are you?"

"Ten and a half, sir."

The man studied him a little longer, then strolled along past the others, stopping to point at J.J.. "Who are you?"

"Merrill," J.J. said, trying to look tough. "I'm J.J. Merrill. We're looking for a man called Kim Song."

The man looked at him, not responding.

"Can you help us?" Shawn asked.

The man frowned at him. "Who are *you*?"

"Shawn Howard," Shawn said.

"We're brothers," Bobby volunteered. "We're looking for our fathers, we — "

Shawn cut him off. "Don't tell him anything."

The man looked at each of them in turn, his eyes pausing on Adrian. "Then, you are Phillips," he said slowly, and looked at Max. "And *you* are Rothman."

Max stared at him, amazed. "*What*?"

The man nodded. "Your father is looking for you. For all of you." He smiled at their stunned reactions. "*I* am Kim Song. The Admiral Rothman said you would try to come here. I do not believe you have done this. But you have." He shook his head. "Incredible. *Incredible*!"

Adrian was the first to find her voice. "Then you'll help us?"

Kim Song shook his head. Sadly. "I cannot help you. I will take care of you and get you back home."

"We're not *going* back home," J.J. said, his fists tightening.

Seeing this, Max stepped in front of him. "You really shouldn't pay attention to my father," he said, in a very friendly voice. "My parents are extremely over-anxious people, see, and — "

"You honor your fathers by this bravery," Kim Song said.

Adrian scowled at him. "So *what*, if you won't help us!"

Kim Song looked very sad. "I'm sorry, you have risked your lives for nothing. You are too late."

Shawn spoke for all of them. "Why? What do you mean?"

Kim Song sighed. "At dawn, your fathers will be moved to P'Yongyang Prison. *No one* leaves there."

"Okay," J.J. said. "Then we have to do it tonight."

Kim Song just shook his head. "It is impossible."

Adrian rubbed her peasant sleeve across

her eyes, close to tears. "Don't you understand? Our fathers could *die*!"

Kim Song sighed, then nodded, moving to the equipment bank. He picked up an 8mm videotape, inserting it into a VCR. "Here," he said. "I will show you this."

The tape was crudely shot, a hand-held image that appeared to have been recorded from a cart of some kind, canvas flaps occasionally obscuring the image. It showed the exterior of a heavily guarded military compound: high walls, barbed wire fences, guard towers, and machine gun emplacements.

"That's where they're holding them," J.J. said, in both horror and awe.

The massive gates to the compound opened, the camera moving inside to a courtyard where stern-faced guards kept watch over a flow of peasants bringing supplies into the compound, and over workers who were lashing cardboard cylinders to bamboo scaffolding.

"Fireworks?" Max guessed.

Kim Song nodded. "Yes. The Workers' Celebration."

The camera flashed by several heavy trucks parked against a wall. Then, a massive water tank attached to a one-story building appeared on the screen and nearby, the circular covering of a well.

"There's the well," Shawn said. "Just like in the plans."

Kim Song looked at him curiously but didn't say anything.

The camera moved on toward a fenced-in area. Someone approached the cart as if an exchange was being made. A door beyond the fences opened and the prisoners, dressed in black pajamas, came into view.

J.J. and the others stared at the tape, stunned by the sight of their fathers looking weak and bedraggled. Adrian inhaled sharply as her father stumbled, Shawn's father bending over quickly to help him up. The men were pushed on by the guards, disappearing through another door.

"Interrogation room," Kim Song explained.

A guard approached the camera, gesturing rapidly with his AK-47. The cart moved on, the tape ending abruptly.

Kim Song sighed and switched off the tape. "Much preparation was done. But without the special rescue force of the Americans, there is no chance. We are too few," he looked at them sadly, "and you are children. I am sorry." He turned to one of the rivermen still in the room, spoke to him in Korean, and turned back as the man left. "Tomorrow we go," he said. "We have a way back to the coast. Until then, you must stay here. That man will show you where to rest — I must go now." He paused. "You have my deep respect. I *am* sorry."

None of them spoke as he left the room,

still stunned by the tape — and by the enormity of the odds that had been against them.

As night fell, they were given a room to themselves, along with blankets and food. They sat on the floor, toying with the bowls of rice, all of them exhausted and defeated. The room was almost dark, lit by an oil lamp.

"Anybody asleep?" Adrian asked finally.

"No," J.J. said, his voice flat.

Adrian let out her breath. "I can't believe it's ending this way."

No one said anything.

"We did the right thing," Shawn said, after a while, and sighed. "We were so close."

More silence.

"I think we were" — Max mimicked Kim Song — " 'incredible!' "

No one smiled, or even responded. J.J. sat with his hands over his face. The room was quiet, except for the sounds of the river outside and the distant tinkling of wind chimes.

A small, determined voice came from the corner. "*Dad* wouldn't quit," Bobby said.

They all looked over at him.

"We can still do it," he said. "Everything's ready. We've still got a boat, all the stuff. . . ."

Adrian's expression brightened. "And we know the way in."

"And the way out," Max said, starting to smile.

"All right, Bobby!" Shawn said.

"One small thing," J.J. said before anyone could get too excited. "We don't have Kim Song and his men. The plan won't work without them."

"We'll improvise," Adrian said confidently.

"Oh, yeah?" J.J. said. "How?"

"Well," Max spoke slowly, "there're those fireworks."

"What," Shawn asked, "the Workers' Celebration?"

"Yeah." Max smiled. "We could celebrate a little early."

"Hey, yeah!" Bobby said.

Shawn motioned for him to be quiet. "What do you have in mind, Max?"

Max shrugged, still smiling. "I don't know. *Yet.*"

Shawn sat back, thinking the whole thing over. "I don't know, maybe we *could* work it out."

Adrian reached over to touch J.J.'s arm, realizing that he hadn't spoken yet. "What do you think?"

"I don't know," he said, looking at his watch. "We've only got three hours until dawn." Then, he grinned at all of them. "Let's go for it."

Chapter 19

They had to work fast: reloading their duffel
bags with tools, radios, and ropes; adjusting
carabiners and climbing harnesses; checking
and re-checking the photocopied Phoenix
plans. Then, pushing out several clapboards
at the rear of the building, they slipped
through the narrow opening and out into the
night.

Disguised in their peasant clothes and hats,
they crossed over a bridge, moving quickly
into the darkened streets and alleys of the
floating city, and into the maze of houses.
They walked swiftly, heading for the out-
skirts of town and the rocky cliff rising
forebodingly toward the clouds.

* * *

When they made it to the top of the cliff —
a long, tiring struggle — they were on a wide,
marshy plateau. The prison camp was set
against the imposing peaks of a distant
mountain range, illuminated by floodlights.

They hid behind a cluster of rocks, near a
tiny shanty-town settlement, inhabited by
workers and farmers who tended to the needs
of the prison. Silently, they stared at the
seemingly impenetrable walls of the prison.
Then, J.J. motioned with his hand and they
crawled over the rocks, slithering across the
mud and marsh grasses, toward the settlement of dilapidated shacks.

Somewhere, a dog barked, a Korean voice
commanding it to stop. They all froze, duck-
ing down in the tall grasses. There was a
clapboard shed with a tin roof in front of
them and Max pointed at it, then at his map.
They all nodded, moving silently toward an
overgrown brick drain cover next to it.

Shawn and J.J. went first, on their hands
and knees, past several restless, tethered
farm animals. They dug around the sides of
the drain, then gripped the edges, heaving it
open. J.J. shined his flashlight down the hole,
revealing a square access chamber below,
with two drain tunnels leading off it. He
dropped down inside, looked around, and
signaled to the others to come after him.

Shawn gestured to Adrian, who quickly

entered the hole, Bobby and Max right behind her. Shawn lifted the cover, taking one last look around, noticing the sky just starting to brighten behind the mountains. He shuddered and climbed into the hole, closing the cover.

They stood in the dirt chamber, flashing lights into each of the tunnels. One sloped away downward; the other led off horizontally in the direction of the prison.

"Which way?" Shawn asked.

"Has to be there," J.J. said, and stepped into the horizontal tunnel, the other four following him.

They walked around a bend in the tunnel, coming to the opening of a masonry collection basin, half-filled with swirling water. Directly across from them, near the domed ceiling, water was pouring out from a large drain tunnel, cascading into the cistern. Then the water seemed to flow from the chamber via a tunnel, the top of its arch just showing above the water. The water was swiftly sucked down the tunnel, indicating a stepped incline beyond. Halfway up the walls, rimming the cistern, there was a narrow ledge, six inches wide.

Max shined his flashlight on the swirling water below. "Okay, how did they plan to get across *this*?"

J.J. looked at the ledge, then removed a coil of rope from his duffel bag. He wound one end around his waist, handed the rest to Shawn, and moved out onto the slippery surface of the ledge.

"Be careful," Adrian said anxiously.

J.J. nodded. Flat against the wall, fingers gripping crumbling gaps in the brickwork, he inched his way around, Shawn slowly playing out the rope.

"See?" he said. "No prob — " One of the bricks he was standing on crumbled, and he fell into the water. Gasping, he tried to stay above the surface, but the current sucked him underwater.

"*Do* something!" Adrian said, trying to help Shawn as he frantically pulled on the rope, which went limp, the other end flying out of the water.

They stared down at the water, too horrified to speak. Then, Shawn started to take off his peasant shirt.

"Look," he said, "I'll go in there and — "

"No!" Bobby grabbed his arm. "Shawn, don't! You'll get — "

Abruptly, on the far side of the tank, J.J. burst to the surface, choking and spitting out water. He grabbed at a steel ladder, then grinned over at them.

"Like I said," his voice was weak, "no problem."

With a sigh of relief, Shawn tossed the end of the rope over to him. J.J. knotted it firmly to the ladder, with Shawn knotting his end to a metal support in the tunnel.

Then, one at a time, they pulled themselves across, hand over hand. Shawn was the last one over, joining the others at the top.

"Leave the rope?" he asked, out of breath, and Max nodded.

They moved along the tunnel, water showering over them, into another smaller chamber, which led to a sloping tunnel.

J.J. paused, seeing steps leading down the slope. "Should be around here somewhere."

Adrian shined her light on some boxes stacked in the corner of the chamber. "There it is."

They ripped opened the boxes, noisy in their haste.

"All *right*," Shawn said. "Smoke canisters and grenades."

J.J. nodded. "Kim Song. So far, so good."

They loaded their bags with the tear gas and smoke grenades, then hurried down the slope, finding themselves at the end of the tunnel, where iron bars across the exit had been forced apart.

J.J. knelt, looking into a deep well shaft leading upward. "This is it," he whispered. "They're right above us."

One by one, they stepped through the bars, grabbed onto a steel ladder, and climbed up the well shaft. At the top, J.J. pushed the drain cover open, and Shawn and he peeked out.

They saw the massive courtyard and surrounding walls, bright under the floodlights, and empty except for patrolling guards by the parapet walls.

J.J. took a deep breath and hopped outside, helping the others out, then lowering the cover back on. He pointed, and they ran silently toward a corner, jumping down into a sunken stairwell.

"Still glad you came?" he asked Bobby; all of them were out of breath.

Shawn lifted his head to peer over the top of the stairwell. "Look at *that*," he whispered.

Max peered over, too. "We're right in the middle of an *army*."

"They're asleep, don't think about it," J.J. said quickly. "Where are the radios?"

Max opened his kit bag, distributing headsets as J.J. glanced up at the far skyline of the prison. The dawn light was brightening on the distant mountains. They didn't have much time.

J.J. put on his headset. "Everybody ready?"

Adrian took Bobby's hand. "Bobby, you come with me."

"Okay," Shawn said. "Let's move."

They waited as a guard passed into the nearest guard tower, then climbed out of the stairwell, heading for the main building, hugging the walls as they went. They hid in the shadows near the steps leading to the prison terrace, the main officers' building known — on their map — as the Summer Palace.

J.J. nodded at Adrian, who ran off with Bobby, carrying her tear gas and smoke canister-laden pack. A workshop by the main gate had been marked on their map and they ran inside, Adrian waving from the window to signal that they were safe.

J.J., Shawn, and Max moved on, Max breaking off to run to some huge gas tanks by a motor pool. J.J. and Shawn waited to be sure he was safe, then ran up some metal stairs to the upper walls, pausing in the shadow of a guard tower. Above them, a guard stared idly out across the hills, yawning now and then. They ducked lower, running to a rooftop where bamboo frames were stacked, loaded with skyrockets, in place for the celebration.

J.J. lifted a tarp, finding a spool of high-speed fuse. He bound it to the rockets while Shawn threaded a wire cable through the frame and up onto the adjustable rocket cradle. They snaked the fuse lines and cable across the roof, from one set of rockets to the next.

Inside the workshop, Adrian and Bobby kept watch on the courtyard. A door opened in the Palace, a soldier stepping out.

"Freeze," she whispered over her radio, "crossing the courtyard."

By the gas tanks, Max froze, one hand on the metal faucet of a tank, gas trickling out onto the ground.

On the upper walls, Shawn and J.J. flattened themselves on the ground, trying to stay out of sight.

Adrian's voice came over their radios. "Okay," she said. "You're clear."

They moved on, staying low, hiding behind a laundry line full of North Korean uniforms, then running over to a fresh bank of rockets. When they touched the rocket cradle, it squeaked and a nearby guard whirled around.

The guard searched the darkness with his eyes for a long, terrifying minute, then turned away, satisfied. Shawn and J.J. exchanged scared glances, then resumed the task of connecting the rocket banks.

Back at the fishery, the room where the five of them were supposed to be had become so suspiciously quiet that Kim Song had been summoned. He opened the door, discovered that the room was empty, and turned to face his men, his expression absolutely furious.

At the prison, light was starting to roll

across the mountains, creeping toward the compound.

Max, after attaching electric cable to a wire-mesh fence near the actual prison block, ran to the workshop, diving inside, his adrenaline pumping.

A moment later, Shawn ran in, too, breathless with excitement, trailing fuse and cable.

"How much time you think we have?" Shawn whispered.

Max shook his head. "Not much."

As they moved to join Adrian and Bobby, they heard the sound of approaching footsteps. Seeing a figure in a North Korean uniform, facing the courtyard, they slipped further into the shadows.

Suddenly, the figure turned, coming directly for them. They all stiffened, realizing that they were trapped.

Chapter 20

As the figure came closer, they saw that it was J.J., wearing the uniform he had just stolen from the laundry line.

"What do you think?" he whispered, turning to show them how it looked.

"I think you scared us to *death*," Shawn whispered back.

"Oh." He looked guilty. "Sorry."

Adrian checked her watch. "Now what?"

"We just go for it," J.J. said. "Once I get 'em out, I'll signal you on the radio, you cover us with the diversion, and it's across the courtyard, right back here, down the tunnel, and back to Kim Song. He'll have to help us from there." He looked at them, his expression less confident than his voice. "Right?"

He met Adrian's eyes, and since there was no time to say anything, they smiled helplessly at each other. Then J.J. moved to the door, pulling Shawn over with him.

"This is it," he whispered. "You ready?"

Shawn nodded. "Yeah. How you gonna do it? Inside, I mean."

J.J. withdrew the .45 from his belt, cocking it, then placing the weapon inside the tunic of his uniform. "Any way I have to," he said grimly. He placed the radio receiver on his head, covering it with the North Korean uniform cap.

Shawn hesitated, not sure what to say. "Listen — " He put his hand on J.J.'s shoulder. "J.J., I — "

J.J. cut him off. "When I get 'em out, I'll signal. If something goes wrong in there, you just get out of here — you can still make it back to Kim Song's. Just remember, we've got until *sunrise*. After that, it's too late."

Shawn nodded, then hugged him — surprising both of them. "Good luck," he said.

J.J. looked back toward the others. "Take care of them, Shawn."

Shawn nodded. "Take care of *yourself*."

J.J. nodded, glanced around for guards, then sprinted across the courtyard.

J.J. ran to the chain-link fence leading to the prison cells, and bent down, his face dripping perspiration. Then he pulled in a strong breath, adjusted his cap, and stepped out of the shadows, walking slowly toward the door of the cell block guard house.

"Too fast, J.J.," Shawn's voice whispered over his radio. "Slow down. That's it. Easy. You're doing good."

Step by careful step, J.J. walked across the courtyard, the block house seeming a million miles away. The door of the house opened, a guard stepping out. He saw J.J. on the other side of the chain link fence and leaned forward to get a better look.

"The guard," Shawn said over the radio, his voice tight with strain. "He's outside. He's watching you, he — turn your head, that's it. Just keep moving, keep walking."

J.J. kept his eyes on the doorknob of the guardhouse, his shoulders tensed, expecting a challenge from the guard at any second.

"He looked away," Shawn said over the radio. "You made it."

J.J. let out his breath, then reached out to touch the door, not sure what to expect on the other side. He found a long corridor lit by bare bulbs, leading to a door at one end. Softly, he closed the main door behind him, flicking on his radio.

"I'm inside," he whispered.

In the workshop, the others crowded around Shawn's headset, listening to J.J.'s faint voice.

"— Turning it off now," he was saying. "Can't risk the noise."

Adrian took the headset from Shawn. "J.J., please be careful," she said into the mike.

In the hallway, J.J. listened to her voice, feeling very emotional.

"I love you," she said.

"I know," he said into his mike. "Out." He reached down to his power unit, switching it off, putting the headset around his neck. He opened his left fist, looking at the SEAL crest. Then, he took out the .45, moving down the corridor to the other door. He opened it, seeing a staircase leading upward.

There was a catwalk at the top, encircling the large room and below that, lit by harsh floodlights, a row of open-topped cells, covered with steel bars. Beyond the stairs, there was a hallway, providing access to the cell. At the end of the catwalk was a massive steel door, the only way in — or out — of the building.

Silently, he climbed up the stairs, hearing muffled Korean voices from above him and down the hallway. Looking down the catwalk, he saw three Korean guards, two about to go off duty, engaged in conversation. J.J. crouched down on the stairs, not sure what to do next.

Outside, the purple glow of dawn was spreading, the sky now a rosy pink. The bright spot above the distant mountain peaks was the sun.

On the winding mountain road leading to the prison, a small convoy of a jeep and a truck drove slowly. A spit-and-polish North Korean general was in the jeep with three soldiers. The truck contained a driver and a guard. The convoy passed a small look-out station, the guards rising to salute the general.

Rounding a curve, the driver of the jeep had to stop, a peasant blocking the road with a pair of oxen, herding them to the pasture on the other side.

The general rose in his seat, ordering the man to hurry up. The peasant, bowing apologetically, urged the cattle on, prodding them with his staff. When the road was finally clear, the convoy drove on. As it passed the peasant turned to watch them go.

He was one of the men from Kim Song's fishery.

In the workshop, Shawn and the others watched helplessly as light began to spread from the walls into the courtyard. A door opened from the barracks and a small detachment of soldiers marched out to the center of the courtyard, a bugler sounding a Korean version of reveille. Above the guard tower, a soldier raised the North Korean flag.

It was morning.

"Five minutes and this place is going to be jumping," Max whispered. "Something's gone wrong, I know it."

"Shut up, Max," Shawn said, just as nervous. "Come *on*, J.J., hurry it up."

Inside the cell compound, the guard on duty lit a cigarette for a departing comrade, the man stepping out through the door. At last, it was safe for J.J. to move. He crept forward, looking down into one of the cages to his right, where a prisoner was stirring restlessly on his straw mat. The man looked up, and J.J. saw that it was his father. His unshaven face was thin and haggard — but it was his father.

Looking up through the harsh glare of the lights, Commander Merrill saw the shadowy figure of someone hiding a .45 automatic. He struggled to his feet, straining his eyes, realizing that something was about to happen. He listened to hear where the guard was, hearing the metallic slide of the peephole slam shut. He looked at the shadowy figure, then to where the guard must be.

"Hey, you!" he said hoarsely. "Baby-face! Down here. Hey, you!"

The guard turned, the outrage of this breach of discipline showing on his youthful face as he picked up a long bamboo stick, one end sharpened to a point. He walked down the catwalk, looking down at Merrill.

"Yeah, *you*, Baby-face," Merrill said. "Got something for you." He spit at the guard, who slipped his rifle to one side, raising the pole with both hands, looking down for his target.

J.J. sprang out from the darkness, the sound of his feet alerting the guard who spun around to face him. J.J. moved forward, the .45 trembling in his hand.

"Don't move," he said, his voice cracking.

Swiftly sizing up the situation, the guard viciously swung the pole, smashing J.J. across the face and arm, the .45 flying out of his hands and down the stairs. J.J. was knocked to his knees, but before the guard could swing again, J.J. tackled him, driving them both to the floor of the catwalk. As they grappled on the floor, J.J. on the bottom, the guard yanked out his combat knife, ready to kill.

In the workshop, Shawn and Max stared, horrified, at the awakening courtyard. From within the barracks, an order was shouted and another squad of soldiers marched out as cooks brought out steaming pots of gruel from the kitchen area. The soldiers stopped and snapped to attention opposite the terrace steps.

"What are we going to do?" Adrian asked, joining Shawn and Max by the little window.

"It's too late," Max said, "we *have* to go."

"Unh-unh." Adrian shook her head. "I'm not leaving without them!"

"There *isn't* any time," Max said. "We have to — "

"We're not leaving," Shawn said firmly. "Okay? We're *not*."

The prison commandant — a hard-faced man they recognized from Kim Song's tape — marched slowly across the compound, up onto the terrace. He looked at his watch, then stood at attention.

"Looks like he's expecting company," Max said quietly.

J.J. and the guard struggled across the catwalk, nearing the edge. Unable to hold him off any longer, J.J. rolled violently off the edge, pulling the guard with him. They crashed into the top of the cage bars, J.J. managing to pin the slightly dazed man. But the guard was stronger and lunged upward, the knife heading for J.J.'s throat. Grimacing, J.J. tried to hold the knife away but, weak from his exertions, he was slowly but surely losing the fight.

Chapter 21

Suddenly, hands came up through the cage bars, fastening around the guard's neck, crushing him into the bars. The guard went limp, then the hands released, and Merrill dropped to the floor of the cage.

Panting, J.J. rolled the guard aside, looking through the bars into the awestruck face of his father. J.J. extended his hand down into the cage, his father reaching up. Their hands clasped tightly, an explosion of tears flooding Merrill's face.

"*J.J.*," he said, stunned.

The jeep-and-truck convoy drove the last few yards up the road, the prison gates swinging open. The convoy entered, the truck parking near the Summer Palace, the jeep pulling to a halt close to the interrogation center, one wheel stopping on top of the well covering — their planned route of escape.

"That's it," Max said, closing his eyes. "We're dead."

They all nodded, watching the general dismount from the jeep and greet the prison commandant.

There was no way out.

In the cell compound, J.J. ran down the stairs to the cells below. Using the guard's keys, he frantically opened his father's cell door.

His father stumbled forward, still unable to believe what he was seeing. "J.J. — "

"No time, Dad." J.J. handed him the keys. "Get the others. We're going home."

As Merrill opened the cell doors, the stunned SEALs moved out of their cages, and J.J. ran to his post at the upper door, putting on his headset.

"We're out," he said into the microphone. "Do it! Let's go!" The mike seemed to be dead, and he looked down to see the crushed and useless transmitter, damaged in the fight. "Oh, *great*."

Below, the fathers were out of the cells. Knowing that he *had* to signal the others, J.J. ran to the window, pulling a pack of matches from his pocket. Hands shaking, he tried to light one, but the soggy head disintegrated in his hands. He tried another, and another, all of them ruined by his fall into the cistern, leaving him no way to make a signal.

Outside, the general and the prison commandant had completed their conversation, other officers joining them.

"They're going to go in there and get our fathers," Shawn said, so scared that his voice wouldn't work right. "Come on, J.J.!"

One of the officers left the commandant, waving to a small group of soldiers, who marched toward the cell block entrance, on their way to collect the prisoners.

J.J., trying to think, remembered the guard lighting a cigarette and ran over to the limp figure, fishing through his pockets. Finding the lighter, he jumped back to the window, holding the lighter out between the bars, striking it.

From the workshop, Adrian saw the small flame in the cell window and pointed.

"There, that's him!" she said. "Do it!"

Max shook his head. "We can't, it's too late."

"No *way* is it too late," Shawn said, and lit the fuse he'd carried in with him, the fire racing out at twenty feet per second, across the ground, up staircases, up the walls, toward the skyrockets above.

Hearing the crackling fuse, the prison commandant looked up, puzzled. Now, for the first time, he saw that the banks of fireworks were not pointed skyward, but aimed at the courtyard. As he started to cry out, the first bank of rockets erupted into an incredible pyrotechnics display, showering the courtyard with explosions of brilliant color and flame, ear-shattering booms echoing through the prison walls.

The guards and soldiers dove for cover as the courtyard became an inferno of zig-zagging explosions and comet-tails of fire and smoke.

J.J. threw open the door of the cell block, motioning with one arm. "Let's go!" he yelled, and he and the fathers rushed out.

Adrian, throwing smoke canisters into the courtyard with the others, saw J.J. and the SEALs as they appeared on the steps of the cell block.

"There they are!" she yelled.

The courtyard was a mass of confusion; Shawn and Max each threw another smoke grenade. One exploded by the cooking area; the other, fuse still burning, landed by the motor pool.

Then, the canvas on the back of the truck that had escorted the general was thrown aside, six men in dark clothing leaping to the ground. Laden with weapons, they opened fire, cutting down guards, firing a rocket that blew a hole through the chain link fence, blasting through the guard towers. The six men fired their way toward the cell compound, Shawn and the others recognizing Kim Song among the group.

"Do it!" Shawn yelled at Max, who touched off a fuse, sending a final streaking barrage of sky rockets into the air.

"Let's go!" Adrian shouted, and they broke from the cover of the workshop, throwing smoke grenades as they went.

Seeing the commandant aiming a pistol at Kim Song, Bobby yanked the pin from a tear gas grenade, throwing it the way Roger Clements might have. The grenade landed at the commandant's feet, enveloping him in a cloud of smoke.

Kim Song and his men lay covering fire as J.J. and the SEALs raced toward the others. Despite the crazed battle going on around them, they all hugged. Kim Song ran over to them, handing weapons to the SEALs.

"Up the stairs, over the wall!" He yelled.

Weapons in their hands, the SEALs instinctively slipped into combat formation, protecting their children, laying down suppressive fire on their captors as they all ran through the gate to the stairs.

Max, the last one through, pulled the gate closed, then moved to a power switch, throwing it. He ran after the others as they scrambled up the stairs toward the upper walls, guards shooting after them.

Just as a fresh detachment of soldiers emerged from the Summer Palace, the fuse of the smoldering smoke grenade lying by the motor pool ignited the gasoline trickling out of the tanks, resulting in a huge explosion.

Max turned to watch, seeing soldiers reach the closed gate and get thrown back by high voltage shocks when they touched it. He smiled and ran on. As they all climbed over the bamboo scaffolding and wall, soldiers appeared above, firing down on them. J.J. stopped long enough to touch the cigarette lighter to a main fuse, the wall roaring into a protective cloud of smoke, sparks, and flames.

They hit the ground running, looking back to see the wall explode into a spectacular fireworks display, the entire scaffolding a shower of dazzling color as the grand finale portrait of the North Korean leader, U Duc Lo, appeared. The Workers' Celebration had come off!

They ran through the Korean settlement, the villagers staring out from their shacks in awe, stunned by the fireworks, the gunfire, and the sight of Caucasians running wildly past them, soldiers shooting from the walls of the prison.

"Do we know what we're doing?" Shawn yelled at Max.

"I sure hope so!" Max yelled back.

Chapter 22

J.J., who was in the lead, turned, urging them on. "Come on," he said, "this way!"

The SEALs, stopping now and then to fire ground cover, fired questions at the kids almost as quickly.

"*How* did you get here?" Commander Howard panted.

"Somebody had to come and get you, Dad," Bobby said, just as out of breath.

"But, you — who's Kim Song?" he asked.

"Part of the plan to get you out," Shawn called over his shoulder.

"Like 007!" Bobby said.

"What plan?" Adrian's father asked, firing off several rounds.

Adrian stumbled on the rough ground but recovered her balance. "Phoenix, the plan they gave up on."

Looking back at the shooting fireworks, Max laughed. "Hey, Happy Fourth of July!"

Wicks, the other member of the SEAL team, laughed, too. "Independence Day!"

Phillips' run was unsteady, and Adrian helped him up the slippery hillside.

"We had to use Mom's car," she said.

He stared at her, pausing in the climb. "You *drove* here?"

"No," she said, "we stole a smuggler's boat."

"You *what*?" he said, and looked at J.J.'s father.

"I don't believe this is happening," J.J.'s father said, his expression just as incredulous.

Behind them, two jeeps roared through the prison gate in hot pursuit.

"Go!" Kim Song yelled, while he and his men fired at the jeeps.

Shawn and J.J. raised the heavy cover of the storm drain, helping the others drop inside. Kim Song and his men came in last, landing on the floor of the storm drain. Before them was a tunnel leading down the steep hillside.

"Come on!" Kim Song jumped into the flowing water, disappearing from sight down the steep tunnel.

With shouts and war-whoops, the kids and

the SEALs streaked down the slippery, moss-covered water-slide.

"Where's this go?" Commander Merrill shouted to his son.

"You got me!" J.J. shouted back.

The storm drain emerged from the hillside just above a canal near the floating city. Preceded by shouts and screams, the kids and the SEALs burst out from the culvert, landing heads over heels in the shallow water and mud of the canal.

"Hey, that was *cool!*" Bobby said happily.

"This way," Kim Song said.

They picked themselves up, wading to the dirt bank of the canal, then running into the narrow sidestreets of the city. Kim Song led them to an alleyway and a narrow dirt road where an ancient flat bed truck — piled high with crates of live chickens and ducks — was waiting.

"This could end badly," Max said, looking at the crates.

"So what else is new?" Shawn said, jumping aboard.

One of Kim Song's men guided them all to the back of the truck where he had prepared a place for them to hide between the rows of protesting ducks and chickens.

The other rivermen gave their weapons to the SEALs and, without a word, ran toward the pole houses and out of sight. Kim Song jumped into the cab of the truck, flooring the heap, leaving behind a cloud of feathers and smoke as they squealed away.

He drove them to a vast, agricultural plain beyond the city, the ride even rougher as he swerved up an embankment to a service road, the chickens and ducks still violently protesting their abduction. Max, standing up between the cages, pointed behind them.

"Hey!" He banged on the cab of the truck, so Kim Song would hear. "They're coming!"

Rising clouds of dust headed across the plain as the jeeps sped to intercept them.

"We're not going to get far in this thing," Howard said grimly.

Kim Song slowed the truck enough to lean out of his window. "Can anybody fly a plane?"

"I had ten and-a-half hours at flight school," Adrian's father said.

"Good. You're a pilot." Kim Song returned to the wheel, slipping the clutch to a higher gear, the engine straining to comply.

Turning hard, he headed the truck down the sloping shoulder of the main road, heading for the airstrip. The truck bounced crazily over the uneven ground, the group in the back barely managing to hang on.

At the airstrip, MCU pilots were sitting at a table, eating rice and drinking tea. Peasants were loading produce from nearby sheds and farm vehicles into an old dilapidated cargo plane. The pilots and peasants looked up, startled to see the approaching truck.

Merrill, Howard, Wicks, and Kim Song leaped out, firing short machine-gun bursts in the air, the peasants and pilots scattering. Phillips and the kids ran to the open cargo door of the plane, tumbling inside. The others continued to fire, then ran for the plane as Adrian's father started the engine, Adrian sitting right behind him.

Shawn's father stuck his head into the cockpit. "Adrian, get in the back," he ordered. "Shawn," he called down below, "watch your brother!"

Adrian looked at him defiantly, plopping down in the jump seat behind her father. "I'm not leaving him."

"All right, all right," her father said. "Just hang on."

"This is it," Shawn's father yelled. "Get us out of here!"

Adrian's father opened up the throttles, the plane picking up speed, checking the yoke and foot pedals. The control panel was a disaster — several gauges missing, loose wires showing — and the windshield was yellowed and cracked. He shuddered and revved the engines up to full power, hauling back on the yoke.

"Are we going to make it, Dad?" Adrian asked.

"I don't know, baby," he said, readying for lift-off. "I hope so."

Chapter 23

The lumbering antique lifted into the air and
the jeeps on the ground opened fire, orange-
red tracers streaking out. Phillips struggled
to gain altitude, dipping and weaving to try
and evade the bullets.

Slugs tore through the thin metal skin of
the plane, so J.J.'s father and Wicks kept
everyone down. Kim Song's attention focused
out the open door as he tried to read the
attack. Phillips, the strain of flying showing
on his face, yanked back on the yoke and the
plane slowly rose higher in the air.

"We're only ten minutes from the coast,"
Shawn's father said. "You've got to stay
under their radar-coastal guns, missiles
everywhere."

Adrian's father nodded, urging the plane a little higher. "If we can get to those mountains, we've got a chance." He put the plane into a steep right-hand turn, rolling around the point of the canyon, pushing hard on the rubber pedal as the canyon wall rushed toward them.

At the North Korean coastal defense batteries, soldiers were running to take up their positions, manning antiaircraft guns. Other soldiers scanned radar screens, looking for some sign of the escaping plane. Still others scanned the skies and the canyons with binoculars.

The plane thundered along the face of the sheer canyon wall, its belly barely clearing the jagged rocks. It pulled higher, arcing over the summit of the mountain, then leveling off.

Flying over the prison, a gun crew spotted them, tracking its course, firing antiaircraft guns. The bullets hit one of the engines, which burst into flames. Other bullets smashed through the side cockpit window, destroying the instrument panel in a flash of sparks and smoke, fragments raking across Phillips' chest.

Adrian screamed, seeing her father's blood-soaked shirt. "Daddy!"

"You stay put! I'll make it!" He turned to

Shawn's father. "Kill the boost pumps and the fuel on that engine! The extinguisher — red lever, on the right side!"

Howard's hands flew over the remains of the instrument panel, shutting down the engine, yanking the fire extinguisher lever for the other engine.

Adrian's father fought to control the plane, which was listing badly to one side. "Feather that prop, pitch control — there!"

Howard pulled back on the lever, changing the pitch of the propellor blades, easing the drag.

Phillips, his breath coming in rapid gasps, hung on, navigating by what was left of his instruments.

Bobby crawled up to the cockpit, looking terrified. "A-are we okay?"

"Yeah, cowboy, we're okay," his father said, managing to sound calm. "Now, you stay down."

The plane careened wildly over another canyon, the gunnery crew on the ground below trying to get it in their sights. Phillips lowered the plane, flying *beneath* the canyon rim, navigating wing to wing between the narrow rock walls. Gradually, the walls widened, as they got closer to the sea.

In the cargo hold, Merrill and Kim Song were looking out the door as the plane flashed over a silvery strip of beach and then over the rolling waves of the ocean.

"We're going to make it!" Merrill yelled.

In the cockpit, Phillips smiled weakly at his daughter. "You hang on, baby," he said. He flew the plane out over the ocean, keeping low to avoid the North Korean radar.

Shawn's father felt around under the copilot's seat, finding a battered old first aid kit.

"Come here, Adrian," he said, opening the box and examining the contents. "Give me a hand."

Phillips flew on, working to keep the plane level, as Howard and Adrian bound his chest with gauze from the first aid kit, trying to slow the bleeding.

"I'm okay," Phillips said weakly. "It's not as bad as it looks." He squinted through the windshield, looking for a landmark — *any* landmark.

Adrian looked out, too, over the endless expanse of ocean. "Daddy, where are we?"

He shrugged, immediately wincing. "Must be fifty miles out. Have to, have to turn — south." He eased the plane into a gentle right turn.

Adrian caught her breath as two daggers of silver light roared out of the sunlight and across their path — supersonic jet fighters.

"Dad, look!" She yelled. "Fighters!"

Chapter 24

In the cargo hold, near the backfi Bobby was the first of the kids to see the jets.

"You guys, look!" he said.

Max leaned over, peering through a bullet hole. "Don't worry, they're ours."

They all grouped around the window, seeing the sleek profiles of two Navy jets, armed with air-to-air missiles.

"*Worry*," Shawn said. "They're warning us off — think we're North Korean."

Bobby's eyes widened. "Will they shoot us?"

"Come on, hurry up," J.J. said, indicating a small bank of windows. "Let's go over there, let them see who we are."

They scrambled over there, falling on produce crates, waving at the windows.

"We need to show them something," Merrill said as he, Wicks, and Kim Song joined them. "Something American."

They looked around frantically, all garbed in peasant clothes or prison uniforms.

Then, Bobby grinned. "I've got it," he said.

Seconds later, they had a forward hatch open. Bobby waved through it while J.J. and Shawn held onto his legs, standing on the ladder below.

Frowning in disbelief, the pilot of the nearest jet eased over, coming in for a closer look.

Waving with one hand, Bobby tore open the front of his peasant tunic, revealing a Bruce Springsteen "Born in the U.S.A." T-shirt.

In the F-14, the pilot and his radio operator stared at the incredible sight of Bobby and the others waving at them. The pilot picked up his radio microphone.

"Cobra, this is Six-gun," he said. "We have vectored primary target, having visual contact — " He paused. "You're not going to believe this!"

As the jets pulled in closer, scrutinizing the plane, Bobby and the others waved and yelled all the more. One of the pilots gave them an enthusiastic "thumbs-up" and the jets pulled ahead, wig-wagging their wings and turning away to the east.

Everyone in the cargo plane went wild with relief, shouting and pounding each other in the back, Shawn pulling Bobby over into a big hug. Max jumped on them, hugging, too.

"We did it!" He yelled. "We *actually* did it!"

On the other side of the open cargo hatch, Merrill and J.J. looked at each other, both beaming with pride and emotion. Merrill wedged the machine gun he'd had ready into a bulkhead and stepped across the hold, embracing his son.

"Partners?" he said.

J.J. smiled. "Yeah, partners."

To prepare for an emergency landing, Wicks and Kim Song strapped Shawn and the others into the cargo netting, while Merrill moved up front to see if he could help.

Phillips sat in the pilot's seat, struggling to maintain consciousness, his reactions groggy. Strapped in themselves, Howard and Adrian watched him worriedly. As the plane broke through the low clouds, they saw the incredibly welcoming sight of the rocky South Korean coastline.

"We made it," Adrian's father said with a tired smile. "All I have to do now is get this crate on the ground."

"Did they, um," Shawn's father coughed, "teach you how to land?"

"I think they said *any* landing's a good landing." He clenched his teeth, shaking with the effort of remaining conscious as he banked from the sea toward the land. He glanced down at the fuel gauge, seeing that it now read empty, the engine beginning to sputter out.

Howard and Merrill exchanged glances; Adrian just plain closed her eyes.

"Well," Phillips said, with the slightest note of hysterical laughter in his voice. "I hope we're all strapped in." Seeing the landing strip at the Nae-Ri Naval Station, he banked hard, heading for the base.

On the airstrip, a crowd had gathered in front of the main hangar, all watching the sky. Mrs. Howard, Mrs. Phillips, and Admiral and Mrs. Rothman all stood very close together, waiting and praying.

Without power, the plane wooshed down, Adrian's father deadsticking it toward the main runway.

"Can't let it rise or fall," he mumbled, trying to stay conscious. "Got to hit it right on. Stay on it."

Commander Howard reached over, squeezing his arm. "Hang on, pal, we're almost there."

The plane rushed forward toward the field, in a wobbling, bucking approach, and with a supreme effort, Phillips leveled the plane out over the field. Then, the aircraft lurched off to one side, sliding off the glide path.

Adrian gasped, seeing her father slumping down in his seat, unconscious, as the blacktop of the field rushed toward them. She screamed, lunging forward to grab the yoke, pulling back as hard as she could as the painted lines of the runway filled the windshield.

The huge crowd by the hangar watched in horror as the plane went into a ground spin, splattering the fire-retardant foam. The landing gear collapsed, the plane spinning completely out of control as the props dug into the pavement, sparks and debris flying through the air.

"Oh, no!" Adrian's mother screamed. "No, not now!"

The plane swung around and around, before sliding and crashing into a plowed field at the end of the strip. The nose shuddered into the soft earth, finally coming to rest.

There was a second of stunned silence, then the fire crew raced toward the aircraft, spraying it with foam as rescuers leaped into the plane.

The forward doors opened, and a dazed and shaken Max appeared, followed by J.J., and

Shawn holding Bobby in his arms. Wicks and Kim Song climbed down, helping Merrill and Howard lower the injured Phillips to the ground. Adrian was next, assisted down by a burly sailor as a crew of emergency medical personnel raced over, ambulances and security vehicles right behind.

Seeing the kids and the SEALs, the crowd erupted into a thunderous cheer, surging forward to greet them. Except for Phillips, who was assisted by Adrian and a corpsman, the SEALs all walked proudly toward the crowd, unassisted, back to freedom.

Max was swept up by his tearful mother and father, while Kim Song, Merrill, and J.J. grinned widely at the scene, their arms around each other's shoulders. Mrs. Phillips, sobbing, clutched at both her daughter and her husband, all of them hugging as he was lowered onto a stretcher. Mrs. Howard ran to hug her husband and sons, all embracing as one.

As they moved forward into the crowd, Shawn lifted Bobby high in the air. Bobby grinned, raising both arms in a victory salute.

"We made it!" He yelled. "We made it!"